SOMEONE LIKE *Me*

MARIAN L. THOMAS

This book is a work of fiction. Names, characters, places and incidents either are the product of the author's imagination or are used fictitiously, and any resemblance to actual persons, living or dead, events, or locales is entirely coincidental.

Printed in the United States of America
Paperback Print ISBN: 978-1-953910-33-2
eBook ISBN: 978-1-953910-34-9

Library of Congress Control Number: 2021903424

Published by DartFrog Blue, the traditional publishing imprint of DartFrog Books.

Publisher Information:
DartFrog Books
4697 Main Street
Manchester, VT 05255
www.DartFrogBooks.com

Join the discussion of this book on Bookclubz. Bookclubz is an online management tool for book clubs, available now for Android and iOS and via Bookclubz.com.

*In loving memory of
Uncle Alvin, Angela, and Winston.*

"You can't go back and change the beginning, but you can start where you are and change the ending."
— C.S. Lewis

Prologue

Y ou started as an assignment for me, but became my way of
life—a daily task that wouldn't let me rest unless I'd shared my
innermost thoughts, be it at two in the morning or eight in the
evening. You have been my savior on dark and lonely nights.

You have been like a second mother, allowing me to tell you everything that happened during the long hours of the day, everything that
ripped my heart open with joy and laughter, or pain and tears.

No judgment you gave, only a listening ear to my scribbling. My
wild talk.

Frankly, I don't know if I would have survived this year without you.

I can't say that I love you; you are not a person, although I suppose
one can love a thing, too.

So I say to you, my dear journal, thank you.

You have been a good friend and my closet, as Jack once said.

Thank you for understanding. For understanding everything.

Even today, as I sit here with only minutes left to write in you, you
understand why I'm wearing this dream of white and lace, and why the
person I gave my heart to told me that he could love...*someone like me*.

Chapter One

May 24, 1985

W e're under the stars, blending in with the black sheets covering the sky—or so I hope. Zee sits next to me. Both of our hearts racing. Zee's eyes staring into mine like he's checking to see if the bones in my body are strong enough to do what he's asking me to do.

Rob Mr. Johnson's gas station.

"What if we get caught?" I ask him, trying to hide the fear in my voice and knowing I haven't put on the big-girl panties required for a task such as this.

Zee laughs, but I, of course, don't get the joke.

"Relax, we ain't gonna get caught. I got this thing completely figured out, baby. Besides, if we don't do this, how are we gonna pay rent this month? Mr. Johnson ain't giving me my job back. That old man fired me for something I didn't even do, so the way I see it, I'm simply giving him a real reason for firing me."

"We can find another way to pay the rent, Zee. Let me get a job," I plead.

"You don't need a job, and you're barely legal anyway. If anyone finds out that I got an eighteen-year-old living with my thirty-five-year-old behind, I'll get locked up just because of that. You understand what I'm saying?"

"I guess."

"Look, ain't I been good to you these last six months?" He places a finger on my lips and slowly trails it down to my heart. "Ain't I been taking good care of you since I found you on the streets after your mama died? I mean, you ain't had to dig in no trash cans or sleep on those cold benches since you been with me, right?"

Zee always goes there, reminding me that he rescued me from Georgia's mean streets. Most times, I feel like I'm his maid, cooking and cleaning like a Hebrew slave after his boys come over and wreck the place—a one-bedroom apartment in a building with more holes in the wall than a poor girl's shoes.

"Zee, you know I'm grateful."

He looks at me with one eyebrow raised, not fully convinced of my sincerity.

"Look, Mýa, I can't pull this thing off without you. I need my girl to have my back. You're my girl, right?" He grazes the side of my cheek with the warm tips of his fingers. "You love me, don't you, Mýa?"

I nod slowly, but I know my heart would have answered quite differently.

"That's my girl. And since you ain't shown that you love me in the way I want, I figure this is your chance to prove it."

"What's that supposed to mean?"

"You know what I mean, but we ain't got time to go into that. Just know that I ain't gonna wait forever. I'd hate to see you end up back where you came from." Zee leans over and places his chapped lips on mine. "Let me go get this rent money."

I try to force a smile, like the moon sometimes does when the air is just right. I swear you can see it smiling even when everything below it is a mess.

Zee looks out his window to check our surroundings once more. "It's two in the morning, so there shouldn't be much traffic. Do me a favor and keep your pretty little hands on that steering wheel and the car running, okay?"

My knees tremble as a couple walks past the car. Zee sits up in his seat, but quickly relaxes when he sees that neither of them glance in our direction. The moment they turn the corner, he opens the glove compartment.

I gasp in horror. "Please tell me that's not a gun!"

"It ain't a toy."

The sweat from my forehead begins to drip down my temples. "What in the world do you need with a gun?"

The sly smirk on Zee's face makes me feel like a five-year-old girl. "What did you think I was gonna use to rob the place, my finger? That kind of thing only happens in movies or white neighborhoods. This is Decatur, baby. It most def ain't Beverly Hills. Besides, the old man keeps a gun right under the register, so I had to come prepared."

"What if—?"

"Stop it, Mya! I ain't got time for twenty questions," he snaps as he slams the glove compartment shut. "Look, the car is stolen, and the cops may be out looking for it, so we gotta do this now."

I can feel the tears falling as I watch him hold the gun like he knows every inch of it with a certain familiarity.

"I'm sorry, baby. I didn't mean to rage out on you like that. It's just that I need us both to be at the top of our game. Can you do that for me?"

Before I can say anything else, Zee jumps out of the car and slips the gun into his coat pocket. It's eighty degrees outside. Anyone would wonder why he's wearing a coat.

Anyone. Especially Mr. Johnson.

I get out of the car and run toward the store window, hoping to get Zee's attention and maybe stop him.

But it's too late.

I am too late.

The next few minutes happen in slow motion.

A young man runs up to Zee and tries to grab him and the gun at the same time.

Shots are fired. From Zee's gun. From the one Mr. Johnson keeps under the register.

Blood covers the twenty-year-old, white and black tiled floor of the store.

Three hearts stop beating.

I don't have my mama's Vaseline to heal any of them.

Chapter Two

T he bulky police detective with a receding hairline glares at me as I sit in a chair, staring at a spot on the wall behind him. I need that spot to help me focus, or maybe I need it to help me forget what I saw. But how can I? How can I forget the screams?

From me.

From Zee.

From the darkness that came afterward.

"Those tears aren't going to save you, little lady," the officer says matter-of-factly.

I don't like him, but then again, I'm not supposed to. Apparently, the feeling is mutual.

"I don't want them to," I finally say without wiping the tears away.

"I want to know what you were doing with a thirty-five-year-old man." He slaps a photo of Mr. Johnson on the table in front of me, forcing me to see the life that Zee took.

I shove the picture back toward him. "He was—"

"He was what? Your boyfriend?" the other detective asks. He's younger than the bulky one, but not by much. The black mole on his cheek has hair sticking out of it, and his thick eyebrows don't move with his eyes.

I nod.

The younger detective stands and leans across the table. "You're an eighteen-year-old kid. I have a daughter your age."

I find my spot on the wall again, behind the fat one—the place where I can see Zee, as he was before all of this. I can see his big, hazel brown eyes staring back at me just before the life left them.

"I didn't know," I whisper.

"You didn't know what?" the bulky one asks. The heat from the room causes sweat to surface around his armpits and stain his shirt. "You didn't know that he was going to rob the place?"

"I didn't know that he had a gun."

"But you knew he was going to rob the place?" the young one fires off as he plants his angry expression in front of my face to get my attention. I can feel the heat of his breath as our eyes meet.

"I didn't know at first. It wasn't until after we were there that Zee told me what he was going to do. Zee said we had to do it so we could pay the rent," I say, frantically searching for my spot on the wall again.

The bulky detective slams his hand down on the table and makes it shake. "People lost their lives tonight, young lady. And for what? So that you and Zee could pay the rent?"

I don't respond.

"Stop looking at that freaking wall and answer us! This isn't a game. We want answers, and we want them now!" The younger detective stands and moves so that my view of the wall is blocked, but at this point, it doesn't matter. Nothing does.

"I didn't want to do it!" I spit. "I tried to tell Zee that I could get a job. I got out of the car to try to stop him."

"So you want us to believe that this was all Zee's idea? Even the gun?" The bulky one roars back as he produces a picture of Zee's gun with yellow and black evidence tape around it.

"I didn't know he had that gun! It wasn't like Zee said, 'Hey, baby, I've got a gun'!"

I can feel the heaviness of the sorrow that's upon my face. I can feel my insides burning up in pain. The ache in my chest is suffocating me. When I look down at the floor, all I see are bullets by my feet.

That's when the tears come down so hard, it's as if someone turned on a faucet.

The younger officer shoves a box of tissues in front of me and says, "Wipe your face."

Someone knocks on the door and hands the bulky detective a yellow envelope and a glass of water.

"Here," he says as he places the water in front of me. "Drink that. It may help you calm down. We're not done here yet."

I don't touch the water as he thumbs through the yellow folder with Zee's real name on it—Zephaniah James Crawford.

"Your thirty-five-year-old boyfriend had quite the record. Did you know that?" the bulky one asks as he places the folder down on the table.

I shake my head.

"None of it is pretty," the younger one says as he picks the folder back up and begins to provide me with a page-by-page summary of Zee's past.

The first page tells the story of a black male with hazel eyes and brown skin who lived in foster homes until he was thirteen.

The second page gives vivid details of how, by the tender age of fifteen, Zee had been arrested four times for petty theft.

The third page outlines how Zee was later arrested for auto theft and, as a result, spent the next two years in juvie.

The fourth page was one I title "Chances." It tells of the journey of a young man who struggled to make a new life for himself. Twenty-four and out on probation, he found that no one was willing to give him a chance, so he went back to what he knew—stealing.

The following pages describe a boy who became a man with a streak or two of gray in his hair, and who continued to bounce in and out of jail until an older man named Mr. Johnson gave him a job at his gas station and a dry floor in the back of the store to sleep on.

At the age of thirty-three, Zee was finally able to sign a lease on his first apartment. The building was old, the floors in the hallway were caving in, and the rats should have paid rent, but Zee called it home because it was his.

Two years later, while walking home from work on a brisk and rainy Saturday night, Zee found an eighteen-year-old girl digging in a trash can, looking for food. She had no coat. She had lost her mother and was living on the streets.

That last part isn't in the folder.

That is in my heart.

Chapter Three

May 24, 1994

I t's hard to believe nine years have gone by since that night—the night that shaped every thought and every emotion that I have had since then. As my feet dig deep into the soft spring grass, I can feel my heart beating like it wants to come out of my body and run butt naked down the street screaming.

This feeling isn't new.

For the past four years, I've been coming here on this date—May 24—right after my waitressing shift at Jack's Pancake House ends. The first time was on a Friday in 1990: the day that I finally inhaled the crisp, fresh summer air as my feet landed on the free side of a facility that had desperately tried to suck the life out of me for 1,835 days.

I can't forget the way the tears streamed down my face as I got my first taste of liberation when I peered into the place that was once Mr. Johnson's gas station, now a hair salon on one side and a barbershop on the other.

Even now, I can still feel the weight of those tears.

I desperately want today to be different. Today, I want to finally do what I've been struggling to do—forgive myself. A counselor once told me that I needed to forgive myself if I wanted to move forward in life. Not that she was wrong, but she had said it so casually; it sounded rehearsed, like something she said to all the young, dumb girls who sat on her couch and struggled to put their bad decisions behind them.

But how can I go on when everyone who lost their lives that night can't? They are gone, and although I didn't pull the trigger, I know I should have done more to stop what happened to them.

As I close my eyes and allow a gentle breeze to soothe my bones, I can still see Zee with the gun in his hand, pointing it at Mr. Johnson. I know that no matter how hard I try to forget it, I will never be able to rid my nightmares of the look on Mr. Johnson's face as the bullet entered his heart.

But the part that horrifies me more is seeing the body of the young man that tried to take Zee down.

He was someone's son.

His name was Daniel Montgomery.

He was eighteen at the time of his death.

I still remember the letters that I wrote to his family and to the Johnsons. All two hundred and forty-one words took me three hundred and twenty painful days to write.

Hello.

You don't know me, but I was there.

I was there the day you lost your loved one, the day a bullet took the life of someone who held a special place in your heart—in your life.

Words can't express the depth of how sorry I am.

I know my sorrow will never be as deep as your own, but if knowing that I regret that night provides even a small measure of comfort to you, I wanted to give you that.

It's not much. Nothing can replace a life.

You're probably wondering if I knew what was going to happen that fatal night.

To be honest, I didn't know much. I didn't know that a robbery was going to occur until minutes before it happened.

I didn't know there was a gun.

I could tell you that I never wanted any of it to happen, and while that's true, I also know that I didn't do enough to prevent the tragedy that occurred.

I will never shed as many tears as you have, but know that mine have fallen just about every night since then.

Even as I write this, I feel them.

I am not asking you to feel sorry for me. You don't owe me that. You don't even owe me forgiveness, but I'll still plead for it, knowing I may never forgive myself for the role that I played in this.

I am genuinely sorry.

It took another forty days, three hours, and ten minutes or so for me to get them to the accountability letter bank, secretly hoping that they would somehow be undeliverable.

Chapter Four

I can't sleep. I sit on the edge of my bed and stare into the darkness of my bedroom, which features nothing more than a bed and a small dresser. My apartment is small, but functional. I don't have much, but I feel I have all that I need.

There's a table and two chairs in my kitchen. My faithful record player takes up a small amount of space on top of an entertainment center that a neighbor gave me just before she was evicted. My black and white television barely works and requires pliers to change the channels. The only thing of value in my apartment is my vinyl record collection.

I check my clock and see that it's just past midnight.

It's on nights like this that I find myself straining to hear them: the midnight cries from women who once slept in nearby beds, all longing for something to rest their heads on that wasn't soaked in urine.

The silence that fills the air around me now is still taking me some time to get used to.

I know I'm supposed to be happy.

My court-appointed attorney told me so.

He tried to convince me that I could find happiness in the arrangement he had made with the court—five years in what they called a women's diversion program since I was considered a first offender. The diversion program relocated me somewhere in the country with nothing but red Georgia clay to look at, a small house with ten beds shared by twenty women to live in, and daily meetings that were supposed to rehabilitate me and get me ready to go back out into the land of the living again.

The land of the living. Back then, I wondered how I was supposed to live after what happened that night. Still, it was either the diversion program or being locked in a prison cell for up to ten years, so of course

I took the country, the shared beds, and the meetings with counselors who said the same things over and over again.

But that wasn't really what I was supposed to find happiness in; that part was supposed to come after I had completed the diversion program and the word "felon" was removed from my legal record. In short, I could go through life without a conviction following my every move. That fact was the only thing that gave me a measure of sanity, knowing that one day I wouldn't have a yellow folder with my full name—Mýa Denise Day—on the front of it.

Not many who lived a life like mine got that chance.

I guess it can also be said that not many have experienced everyday things as I did afterward—things such as smelling the reddest of roses as I walk down a sidewalk, getting a job, or sleeping in a bed upon which no one else has cried.

So, yes, I'm supposed to be happy, but as I sit alone, feeling like the walls are caving in on me, I long for one thing—my mama and her jar of Vaseline. Dorothy Rena Day was the queen of Vaseline. She believed it was the be-all to every ailment.

Including broken hearts and shattered dreams.

The first boy I liked was a white boy. His name was Brian Andrews. He had straight brown hair that he kept combed back, and his eyes were so blue, you thought you were swimming in an ocean when he looked at you. Anyway, when I was in sixth grade, on picture day, I walked over to him with a small bundle of flowers in my hair and my favorite hot pink floral dress on, and I asked him one question. "Could you like someone like me?" In response to my heartful question, he picked up a handful of awful, smelly mud and threw it at me. The mud slid down my dress and fell on my black shoes, the ones with the bows on them.

When I got home, I bathed and then Mama covered my entire body in Vaseline, convinced it would heal my heart because she knew it wasn't the mud, but *why* he threw the mud that had cut me to the core.

Brian Andrews, the boy that I just knew would give me my first kiss, had screamed loud enough for all to hear that he could never like a dumb, dark-skinned girl with nappy hair.

That was integration for you.

—⁂—

I will never forget the day I stood in front of the mirror, staring at myself and wishing I was someone else when Mama came in with her jar of Vaseline.

"That isn't going to make my skin lighter, Mama," I'd snapped at her.

"You're right. It isn't going to make your skin lighter, Mýa, but it will make it shine as beautiful as the person you are on the inside."

When I went to say something sarcastic back to her, she grabbed at her chest.

I was sixteen years old when I realized Vaseline couldn't heal my mama's forty-two-year-old heart.

Chapter Five

Monday morning. The sun hasn't quite opened its eyes as I walk into Jack's Pancake House around five, an hour earlier than my shift requires; Jack gives us our employee meals for free if we eat them off the clock. The place is a family-owned restaurant with crisp white walls that get a fresh coat of paint each year, bright red vinyl booths, and chrome tables that are topped with fresh yellow and white daisies every morning.

Jack Tanner is a tall man with a full head of thick, curly gray hair. He often jokes that most of the men in his family lose all their hair by the age of thirty. Jack is happy that at sixty, he still has his.

I love hearing Jack speak, especially when he's excited about something. That's when I can see the dimple in his right cheek. I have never met anyone with a bigger, more forgiving heart than Jack's. His wife of forty-two years, Mary, often says that Jack's skin is whiter than Alaskan snow, but he doesn't know it.

I agree. Jack could use some sun.

If it weren't for Jack, I would never have gotten the associate's degree with my name on it that now hangs in his office, nor would I have been able to pay for it. Jack and Mary are also the only people who know about my past.

"Twenty-seven is still young, Mýa. You can't wait tables forever. I won't let you. You can do more," Jack yells over the sizzle of bacon being tossed on the grill as I grab my first cup of coffee.

"I don't think I could ever leave you, Jack."

"You can, and you will. You're like this bacon that smells and looks good, but eventually, people do something with it—they eat it. Why? Because bacon is made for more than smelling and looking good. It has a purpose. You need to find your purpose."

I laugh as I place a piece of toast on my plate. "So now I'm a piece of bacon?"

"Better! One day, someone is going to come through those doors, look into those big, beautiful brown eyes of yours, and then ask me for your hand in marriage."

"Just like that, huh?"

"It may not happen exactly that way, but you get my point. I don't know the future, Mýa, but I can smell love in the air, and it's going to rain down on your unbelieving head."

"I think that bacon grease has you talking nonsense, my friend."

Just as I put a little sugar in my coffee, I hear the restaurant's front door open. Jack looks my way, and both of us move quickly toward the front to see who it is.

Standing there in front of the counter is a handsome young man with three boxes of lettuce in his hands. He looks like he can't be a day older than nineteen.

"I guess I'll have to wait for him to mature a little bit more," I say to Jack with a chuckle.

"Women date younger men all the time. I keep telling some of the girls here that haven't found the 'one' to give it some time. Their husbands just haven't been born yet."

Chapter Six

"Time for you to talk to me, Nina," I whisper as I pull off my apron after a double shift, place my favorite Nina Simone record on the record player, and begin to shake the pancake flour out of my short hair.

Kicking off my shoes, I snap my fingers to the soft melodies of "Feeling Good" as they float through my apartment. Nina always knows how to talk to me. Sometimes it feels like she wrote her songs just for me.

With a glass of wine in my hand, I stare out my window at the Friday night streets of Atlanta. "I need to be out there with them," I say with a heavy sigh as I watch a couple of young girls pile into a small car. Their dresses are so tight that I wonder how they can breathe. But who cares about breathing when you're young and living life, right? Sometimes, I wish I could be that carefree, but I know better. Still, I can hear Jack telling me to get out of my apartment and go live my life. For the first time, I decide to take his advice.

Nina is still belting it out in the background as I pull out my favorite pair of black heels, a red satin dress that I picked up from the Goodwill and that still has the tags on it, and some gold glitter for my eyes.

Feeling good about finally getting out and loving how my red dress rests on my hips, I glance at myself in the mirror and dab a little of Mama's favorite on my lips—Vaseline mixed with a hint of ninety-nine cent red lipstick. I turn off the record player and then grab my purse. The cab arrives just as I make it down the stairs.

"Marco's in Midtown," I say as I adjust my seat belt.

"It's the perfect night for a little jazz and some spoken word, isn't it?" the cab driver asks.

"It is," I say, looking out the window and admiring the bright city lights that flash by us as we head down the expressway.

"I wish I could go into Marco's with you. I'd buy a pretty lady like you all the drinks she wanted," he says, winking at me through his rearview mirror.

I smile.

Twenty minutes later, and after a hundred "pretty lady" comments, I walk into Marco's and absorb the music and conversations as they seep into my skin. I can't lie—the vibe of the place has me feeling grown.

Throughout the club, the electric blue concrete floor is sprinkled with gold flecks, creating the elegant illusion of walking on stars. Large cases framed in gold line the walls, each containing a different musical instrument. My eyes linger for a moment on the lyrics from various jazz songs that are engraved into the white and gold wallpaper that surrounds me on all sides.

My heart flutters as I stand in awe, gazing at a large portrait of Billie Holiday that rests in the center of the glass wall behind the mahogany bar.

I feel like her eyes are staring into mine.

Chapter Seven

T he hostess is pleasant as she ushers me to a small black table with gold legs off the side of the stage. She hands me a drink menu, goes over the drink specialties, and then provides the name of my waitress—Ms. Maggie Estep.

I laugh as I glance over the drink menu and say, "Maggie Estep can't be her real name."

"Every staff member here is named after a musical instrument, a famous singer, or a spoken word artist," she says as she points to her own name tag—Eartha Kitt.

"You do resemble Ms. Kitt," I say, placing the drink menu on the table.

"I get that a lot," she says. She takes my drink order and lets me know that my waitress will be the one to bring it to me.

By the time Ms. Estep places my martini on the table, I'm thoroughly engrossed in the groove of the saxophonist, snapping my fingers to his beat and enjoying the way he made his saxophone do what it was meant to do.

Jack would be proud to see me out, I think as I lean back in my chair and join the swaying heads of the crowd with my own. I can feel my heart thump with each note. Something deep inside me is waking up.

I order another martini and watch as the announcer walks out on the stage and introduces the evening's spoken word artist. His name is Daniel Jacobs. Light and bright with a black suit, white dress shirt, and white Converse shoes, he stands in front of the mic and waits a second or two as the bass player warms up the audience.

His words drip gently from his lips. My eyes roam the audience and I can see their ears opening and their lungs expanding as they breathe in the melodies that he delivers in such a way that it sounds like a jazz beat sprinkled with a dash of his broken heart.

He is intoxicating.

His rhythm is clean and crisp.

He's got me feeling each lyric that moves through the air. I can feel the depth of his pain penetrating down to my gut, causing my insides to mourn because the pain is too familiar. Too raw. All these years, and I can still feel the pain stabbing me.

As I sip on my martini, I realize why I feel like a magnetic force is drawing me to the words in his piece. Pain recognizes pain.

His piece is called "Guess I Always Knew".

I remember the first day I saw you,
sitting there like a tall drink of refreshing Kool-Aid.
You know the kind, the kind only a mama could make,
the kind where the strawberry flavor made my bones shake.
I remember your smile, girl,
teeth glistening like a baby's new white diaper cloth.
A white silk dress hugged your beautiful chocolate neckline.
Your eyes sucked up the sun, dried up the waters, and washed away the loneliness from
my heart.
I remember thinking I was going to make you mine for a lifetime.
It took one day to love you and one day to lose you.
I never told you.
Never told you that I wanted children. Can't say why now.
It seems I never told you a lot of things.
Funny now, now that I want to share my dreams.
I have to admit, girl.
I have to admit that hate boils down in my heart for you.
For him, the man you put your touch upon.
You know—the touch that should have only belonged to me.
It hurt, girl.
No, it burned, girl.
It burned like the fire that was aching in my bones.
The day I put that ring on your finger, you should have only wanted me.

I know I was good enough—tall, solid shoulders filled with endless love.
What more did you want, girl? What little did I give? Too bad you can't answer me now.
Now that you're gone.
Can a man scream?
When I think of you, I hear the screams inside my head.
Seeing you and him in our bed.
Mama could see the real you. She always could.
The side of you hidden underneath the surface.
She saw it in your eyes.
I married you anyway. Walked down the aisle and said, "I do."
I think you whispered something that day.
It wasn't, "I love you."
Guess I always knew.

As Mr. Light-and-Bright walks off the stage, he glances my way, and in the brief moment that our eyes meet across the short distance that separates us, I can feel something tugging at my heart.

Chapter Eight

"**M**orning, Jack!" I shout over the roar of the pancake mixer as I straighten out my apron and make sure my name tag is in place.

"What's up with you?"

From the first day I started working here, Jack has been like a father to me, always knowing when my face is hiding my inner thoughts.

"Nothing," I say quickly. "I just have some things on my mind."

He stops the machine and gives me the once-over.

"Stop analyzing me. I'm good."

"This pancake mix is good; you aren't. Come into my office." I try giving him a reassuring smile, but he isn't buying it. "Come."

Jack's office is like walking into an antique store. Every piece has a connection to his roots. On a table in the corner sits a beautiful statue of a slave breaking his chains that was carved by his grandfather. Jack once told me that every time he looks at the statue, it reminds him of his responsibility to help others. Jack's grandfather was responsible for helping many slaves find their freedom. Every time I look at the statue, it gives me hope. I hope that one day, I, too, will be free. Every day, I feel like the chains of the past have me in shackles.

Jack keeps his eyes on me as he takes a seat behind his cluttered desk. I plop down into a chair that's older than both of us.

"When are you going to get rid of this thing?" I ask jokingly. "I can feel the springs, you know."

Jack laughs. "Never. That chair has been in the family for generations."

"So have the springs."

He grins and claps his hands. "Stop stalling. Tell me what's up."

"I went out last night." I watch his eyes widen. "Before you go there, I was alone."

"Oh. At least you got out. That's a start."

"True," I say as I sit up and cross my legs. "I went to Marco's."

"Really? Good for you. I love that place, and so does Mary."

"I didn't know you were into spoken word."

"I'm not. I love jazz, and Mary loves all the mushy stuff they talk about on stage. I call it a win-win."

"It's spoken word, not mushy stuff."

He throws his hands up in the air. "Tomato, tomahto. Who cares? As long as my Mary is happy."

"Of course she's happy; she has a man like you that's still trying to woo her."

"That's what I keep telling her."

I love the relationship Jack and Mary have. They understand each other and they know how to have fun together.

"You're stalling again," Jack says.

"Okay," I say with a long sigh. "Last night, this spoken word artist performed a piece that reminded me of something I feel like I will never have."

"A man?"

"Sort of. The piece was about being hurt, and it's not that I want to be hurt, but the love the artist once had for this woman…"

"You want that, right?"

"I do. When the artist finished the piece, I could feel that longing tugging at my heart."

"I get it, but love doesn't come when you don't believe in it."

I fold my arms. "I believe in love."

"How can you believe in love when you don't believe in yourself?"

"I believe in myself."

Jack pretends to spit on the floor. "Lies, and you know it."

"How? How am I lying?"

Jack gets up and closes his office door. I watch him as he moves back to his desk, scared because I know what he's about to say even before the words fall from his lips.

"You think I don't know that you think no one will want to be with you because of your past. But it's not just your past that makes you doubt the very essence of love. It's also your skin. I hear you talk about how dark you are. You call that curly hair of yours 'nappy.' How is someone going to love you for you when you can't love all the things that make you a thing of beauty, Mýa? And I'm not the only one who thinks so, you know. Every guy in here stares at you, and you—well, you walk around here like you don't see them staring, and I know that's because you don't see yourself the way they see you. Not as an object, but as a woman. A beautiful, intelligent, black woman who can sing."

I look up at him then.

Jack points at me. "You thought I didn't know?"

"How? How did you know?" I ask.

"I've heard you singing Nina Simone songs when you think no one is around. I told Mary that I wish I knew someone in the music business because that voice of yours deserves to be heard by the world instead of just over pancakes, if you know what I mean." He looks into my tear-filled eyes and smiles. "You've got to raise your head and see all that you have to offer, Mýa. Not too many people can match their inner beauty with their outer beauty, but it comes naturally to you. Stop selling yourself short. I'm not saying you should become one of those people who thinks more of themselves than they ought to, but you've got to think something of yourself. If you don't see your value, you're going to let some man out there give you pennies when your heart is worth hundred-dollar bills. You know what I'm saying?"

The truth hurts, but I understand what Jack is saying. Tears slide down my cheeks as I struggle to control my emotions, but I'm too far gone. I know that the thick layers of hate I have harbored for my skin color need to be acknowledged. It's not that I want to be white. I just don't want to be the flavor of chocolate that no one ever wants—dark. That kind always goes stale in the candy store because little kids want the creamy milk chocolate, or even the more expensive white chocolate.

"I wish it were easy for me, Jack, but it isn't. I want to love myself. I do, but every time I look in the mirror, all I see is the girl that none of the boys liked because her skin was too dark."

"Mýa, from what you told me, you went to a school that was still trying to integrate its students. The other girls were all probably as white as me, but that doesn't mean that your skin was any less beautiful. Listen, kid, you can't let the opinion of others dominate the person you are or who you become. Don't you dare make that mistake!"

The passion I hear in Jack's voice tells me that he's speaking from experience on the matter.

"Who was she?" I ask. Jack's eyes rest on the statue, and for a second, I see pain behind them.

"Her name was Caroline Thomas. She was the most beautiful black girl my seventeen-year-old self had ever laid eyes on. Of course, back then, black people were called 'colored.'"

"What happened?"

"What typically happens when a black beauty captures a white boy's southern heart? Everywhere we went, people fought against us. White people. Black people. Everyone, it seemed. Caroline couldn't handle it. She said love shouldn't be that hard, but I felt that anything or anyone you love should be worth fighting for. I didn't care if I got bruised in the battle. To me, having her as my wife was worth it. That's how my family raised me: to marry who your heart loves. The day I was going to propose, I found out that she had run off and married a boy her family could be happy with—not because he was good enough for her, but because he was black. It broke my heart into so many pieces; it wasn't until I met Mary that it felt whole again.

"She was like a calming wind that blew upon my heart. Her almond-shaped, brown eyes drew me in and told me that I would be okay. I remember the first time she smiled at me; I felt it in my bones. And Mary was beyond beautiful. Her hair was thick, long, and wild. She'd let it hang down her back, and when she walked, it moved like music. All these years later, and my Mary is still beautiful. Her hair isn't as long as it once was, but it still moves like music to me.

"My Mary didn't care that I was a white southern boy, or that she was a beautiful, mocha-colored girl. She only saw me, and I only saw her."

"Mary's parents didn't feel the same way? I mean, they were black, too."

"Thankfully, they didn't. They understood that love has no boundaries, even though the world tries to build them all around us."

I smile. "Jack, I don't think it had anything to do with boundaries. I think you love you some black women."

"There may be some truth to that," he says, giving me a wink.

I find an uncluttered spot on the wall behind Jack, and while the picture is not as clear as it used to be, I can still see Zee's face.

"It's not just my skin, Jack."

"Stop. Before you even go there, you were only eighteen. Young and dumb, the way I see it. You allowed yourself to be seduced by someone who should have known better."

I shake my head. "No, Jack. I wasn't seduced. I knew I should have gotten out of that car sooner and tried to stop him, or walked away the moment he asked me to help him."

Jack leans back in his chair and stares at me. "Why didn't you?"

His question catches me off guard as I lean back in my chair as well, and then mull it over in my mind for a few seconds.

"I guess I was afraid," I finally say.

"Afraid of what?"

"Of having to go back to living on the street. Do you know how many nights I had to fight off every creep that thought they could come at me when the sun went down? Two years. For two years, I lived out of trash cans. I slept in abandoned buildings. I begged for quarters, dimes, and even pennies. I was that kid that everyone passed. Zee was the only one who saw me. He was all that kept me from going back to that life—the life that almost killed me. Not in a literal sense, but in that it tore out everything that I had on the inside. It ripped me open and left my bones dry. That life sucked out every dream I had as a child and made me look at the world as if it were void of possibilities."

I see the tears gathering in the corners of Jack's eyes.

"I get that, but so did Zee," Jack says softly. "That sly buck knew your fears, and he played upon them. As my mama would have said, he wasn't right on the inside. No thirty-five-year-old man worth his salt would have been messing around with an eighteen-year-old."

I look down at the floor. My heart is pounding hard enough to hurt, but I know I have to tell him the whole truth so I can put his mind at ease.

"Jack," I say slowly. "I want to tell you something." He sits up straight as I wipe away the tears and take a deep breath. "In the six months that Zee and I were together, we never did anything but kiss."

His eyes tell me that he doesn't believe me, although his face remains the same.

"It's true," I insist. "Don't get me wrong, he tried—multiple times. But something inside of me always made me pull back, even when he said that I owed it to him."

Jack's face turns red with anger. "As I said, that dirty little creep wasn't right on the inside!"

"Maybe."

"He played the 'if you love me' card."

I let out a long sigh and allow my feet to rest on the floor. "It's funny, but Zee used to tell me that he loved me all the time. When he would ask me if I loved him, I couldn't say no, but in my heart, I knew that I didn't."

"You believed that he loved you."

"I can't say if I believed him or not, but as I said earlier, I needed him. That day that Zee found me, I pleaded for a couch or a floor to crash on. I was so desperate. The rain had been coming down hard all day, and I was tired. Tired of fighting the wind."

"The way I see it, you felt a sense of obligation to Zee because he had taken you in—loyalty, even."

"Perhaps. Zee certainly never hesitated to remind me of that fact." I place my hands in my lap. "There, now you know all there is to know about me."

Jack claps his hands together. "I doubt that. I've been married for over forty years, and one thing I've learned is that a man will never know all there is to know about a woman. Women are like closets. They bring out the things they want others to see and keep all the other stuff buried in a box with a ton of clothes and shoes on top of it. No man is going to go digging in her clothes, so she knows it's safe. She's safe. You're a woman, so you're no different. You may not have as many clothes or shoes yet, but give it time. Life has a way of filling up your closet."

I smile, knowing he's right.

"You know, Mýa, I love talking to you, but have you ever considered seeing someone?"

"You mean like a shrink?"

"I mean like a professional."

"I don't need a shrink, Jack. I have you."

He belts out a strong laugh. "Seriously speaking, I want you to do me a favor."

"What's that?"

"I want you to get a journal."

"I'm too old for a diary."

"A journal isn't a diary. Mary has one. I admit, when I first found out, I was jealous."

"Of a journal?"

"I know that sounds crazy. But when Mary first started journaling, I felt like she was telling it all the things she should have been sharing with me. It wasn't until I saw how much she enjoyed writing in it that I started to get it. That journal is her closet. Mary does her journaling every morning for about fifteen minutes or so. It really makes her feel better and that, in turn, makes me feel better."

I reach over and touch his hand. "I'll think about getting one."

Jack reaches into a drawer. "Here."

I look down at the journal he's handed over. "How long have you had this?"

"Doesn't matter. I want you to use it. Promise me that you will try it."

I placed the journal in my apron pocket. "I'll give it a try tonight."

"Perfect. Now, I better let you get back to work before everyone figures out that you're my favorite."

I stand and head toward the door. "Thank you, Jack."

"Anytime, beautiful."

Chapter Nine

I glance at my clock only to find that it's just past eight. My evening thus far has been rather uneventful. Although I'm tired, my eyes are wide open and searching every inch of my ceiling like I'm going to find the meaning of life hidden under the dingy white paint that's peeling in some places.

Of course, the meaning of life is nowhere to be found, but my eyes do land on a spider resting comfortably in the corner of my bedroom.

"I am bored," I whisper to the spider as I throw the covers off and climb out of bed.

An hour later, I jump into a cab and head toward Marco's, thankful that this time I have a taciturn driver.

A rare July breeze wafts through the backseat as I gaze out the window and enjoy its touch on my skin. I ease back into the black cloth seat, taking in the contemporary jazz the cab driver is humming to.

As we reach Midtown, I imagine what it would be like to live in one of the historic homes that we pass, or to look out from the balcony of one of the apartment buildings and see life moving to its own rhythm below.

When I was younger, my mother and I used to lie on the wood floor of our tiny apartment and pretend that we were living in one of the fancy buildings that I now see in the distance as we get closer to Marco's.

I miss her so much.

Opening my purse, I dab a little Vaseline on my lips.

—‡‡‡‡‡•

I sit at the bar, not wanting to wait the quoted hour and a half for a table. My eyes roam the crowded space, searching for a familiar face as I sip on a Diet Coke.

I spot Mr. Light-and-Bright across the room, sitting in a booth and staring into the eyes of a woman just as light and bright as he is. As I watch them laugh and enjoy the space they occupy together in the tiny booth, I feel my bubble of possibilities pop.

I turn around on my barstool and get a glimpse of myself in the mirror behind the bar. *Who are you fooling? And why did you come here wearing the same old ninety-nine-cent lipstick, hoping to run into him?*

By the time the bartender comes back over, I feel like grabbing my purse and leaving. Instead, I order another Diet Coke after coming to the realization that no one is waiting for me at home except a spider.

Two Diet Cokes later, I feel myself mellowing out and beginning to enjoy the music, the atmosphere, and the fact that I was out and buzzing off caffeine. Do my eyes casually travel across the room once or twice? Yes, but the moment I see Mr. Light-and-Bright kiss the woman who might become the second Mrs. Light-and-Bright, I know it's time to end my stalking foolishness.

"Hi."

The voice causes me to jump slightly. As I turn around, my eyes fall upon the pearly whites of a man who looks like someone has dipped him in a bag of freshly roasted cocoa.

"I'm Michael—Michael Davis. Do you mind if I sit next to you?"

I nod and try to act like the smell of his cologne doesn't have me curious.

"Can I buy you another drink…?" He trails off, looking at me expectantly.

"Mýa," I faintly say, feeling unsure of myself as I grip my Diet Coke in my hands and wishing I had something much stronger.

He places his glass of wine down on the bar, and I pray the dimmed lights overhead will hide how nervous I am.

"Can I buy you another drink, Mýa?"

"It's not a drink."

He looks at my glass. "It's not water."

"I mean, it's not a real drink. It's Diet Coke, but I'd welcome whatever you're drinking."

Shut up, girl. Just stop talking.

As he motions to the bartender, I take a deep breath, inhaling his handsomeness.

"Do you come here often?" he asks as he takes a sip of his wine.

"This is only my second time," I say as the bartender places a glass of wine down in front of me.

"Nice. I'm a first-timer. I heard about this place from a friend."

"A female friend?" The question slips off my tongue and I want to slap myself for asking it.

He grins, and I feel my knees shake.

"I don't have a girlfriend, I'm not married, and I'm not seeing anyone. I'm single, in every sense of that word. What about you?"

Okay, pick your jaw up off the floor.

"Same," I say, adjusting my posture and silently hoping that he can't hear the slight tremble in my voice.

"Cool. I'm glad we got that out of the way."

There's a small wedding venue just down the street. "Me, too," I say as I take a sip of my wine, resisting the urge to take a bigger one.

"This place is better than I expected. The music is inviting, and the spoken word artists are showing out tonight. You write any poetry?" he asks.

I like the way he speaks with his hands. "I don't, but I did start journaling." *Better thank Jack for that one.*

"Journaling, huh? That sounds like a person who's in tune with her needs."

Leave that alone. "Why do you do that?"

"Do what?"

"Talk with your hands? It's like you're spelling out your words."

"Sorry, habit. I used to sign. I haven't done that in a long time. Hope I didn't freak you out."

"You didn't. That's a good skill to have. Did you learn sign language for work or something?"

"I learned sign language when I was young so that I could communicate with my brother."

I catch a familiar hint of sadness in his eyes that tells me why he hasn't used his sign language skills in a long time.

"How long has he been gone?"

"Too long," he says, almost in a whisper.

I take a sip of my wine and will the silence that has slipped between us to leave just as quickly as it came.

"I'm starving," he suddenly says as he stands up. "I came here from work, and I didn't get a chance to have dinner. There's a small diner within walking distance of here. Can I interest you in a plate of pancakes?"

I laugh at how ironic his question is.

"What, you don't like pancakes?"

"It's not that," I say, finally getting ahold of myself. "I'm a waitress at a pancake house downtown, off Peachtree Street. I've been working there for four years. It's close to my apartment."

Girl, he just asked if you like pancakes. You gave him your resume.

"My mother was a waitress, so I have a lot of respect for the profession."

"I've never thought about waitressing as a profession."

"My mother used to say that anything that pays the bills and is legal is a profession." He slaps his hands on the edge of the bar. "Come on, let's go."

I glance around as I stand up and subtly straighten out my dress. I can feel his gaze on me.

"Wow. You're beautiful."

I don't know how to respond to that, so I glance at the floor like there's something unique down there. He grabs my hand, and the warmth of his touch takes me by surprise. I gently pull my hand away.

"I promise I'm not a serial killer or something, and the diner is a five-minute walk from here. You can trust me."

I search his face before making up my mind. "Okay, I'll go."

"Perfect! Then again, I could be a serial killer or something who just lied and said he wasn't so you would go with him."

"Don't worry; I'm not packing pancakes in my purse," I say with a wink.

"Good comeback," he says with a grin as we walk toward the door.

Chapter Ten

"It's beautiful out here tonight. You can see the stars," Michael says as we step outside and begin making our way toward the diner.

"You can," I say, looking up for a second. "I can't believe how warm it still is this late in the evening."

"You looked deep in thought a minute ago. Are you still wondering if I'm a serial killer?"

"Maybe."

"Can I ask you a question?"

"Sure."

"Did you come to Marco's for someone else tonight?"

I look over at him. "That's a funny question to ask."

"I only asked because I saw you when you walked in, and for a while there it looked as if your eyes were fixed on some fellow snuggled up to another woman."

Girl, you're busted.

"So, you were checking me out before you came over to say hello?"

"You say that like you're surprised. I'm sure I'm not the only one who was. I was just probably the first one to act on it."

"I doubt that."

He grabs my hand. "I don't. You're beautiful."

There's a cat just ahead of us trying to cross the street, and I jump at the chance to use it to break up the heaviness of the moment. "I hope that poor thing doesn't get hit," I say as I slide my hand away.

"So, are you going to answer my question from earlier?" he asks.

"I heard him perform before and when he came down off the stage, I thought—"

"That you two had made a connection?"

"Yeah, something like that. Tonight proved that foolishness wrong, though."

"Thankfully."

I glance over at him, surprised by how direct his response was.

"What? I'm just honest." He stops and takes my hand in his again. "Don't pull away, okay?"

My heart thumps at the intimacy. "Okay," I whisper as we begin walking again.

"The truth is, I almost didn't come tonight, but my friend insisted that I get out more. He claims that all I do is work."

The warmth of his hand begins to sink into my skin, and I feel myself relax. "Is he right?" I ask.

"He is, but I'm glad he made me go out tonight."

"Why didn't he come with you?"

"He was going to until his wife went into labor."

"Good excuse."

"I know, right? I told him the same thing."

"What kind of work do you do?" I ask as the diner comes into view.

"I'm an attorney." I feel a spark of nervousness shoot down my spine, but he gives my hand a gentle squeeze. "I'm kidding. I'm far from an attorney. I'm a real estate agent—nothing fancy."

"Do you like doing that?" I ask, feeling my shoulders relax.

"It keeps me busy and pays the bills."

"I can relate to that, except waitressing barely pays mine."

"You ever thought about doing something else? Something you're passionate about?"

"I've been giving that question a lot of thought lately," I say.

"And what did you come up with?"

"It's still a work in progress. What about you? I take it selling homes is not your passion."

"True. It's something I'm good at, but my real passion is photography. There's something special about seeing the world through the lens of a camera."

"Like what? What do you see?"

"I don't know—different things. I see the world's imperfections. I see its beauty, its innocence. Capturing those imperfections and that innocence over the years is what has helped me get through lonely nights."

I give him the side-eye, not really believing those nights have all been so lonely.

"I swear. I haven't dated anyone in years. Not seriously, at least."

As we walk, I admire his broad shoulders, the way his jawline moves in a romantic harmony of ease and confidence when he talks, and his bald head. He's slightly taller than I am—around six feet, I suppose. I glance down at his shoes. Hard bottom. Jack always said a real man wears hard-bottom shoes.

"I would love to see your photos sometime."

"Really? You don't have to say that."

"I mean it."

"Then I would love to show you some of my work one day. One day soon, I hope."

"That would be nice," I say. "Now, I've got a question to ask you."

"Shoot."

"How old are you?"

"Wow. I'm not quite sure where that came from, but I'm thirty. Do I look older or something?" he asks with a smirk.

"No. I was just curious."

"Did you wish I was older? Because I can add a few years if you need me to."

"No," I say with a chuckle.

"Did you wish I was younger?"

"You're funny."

"I hope that's a good thing," he says, glancing across the street.

I follow his eyes. "You see something over there?"

"A bench. Look, I know I said I was hungry, but that seems like a pretty nice park over there and I feel like that bench is begging for us to join it. Do you mind if we take a detour?"

I glance around. "It's getting late, and that park seems pretty vacant."

He moves in front of me, and I feel like his eyes can see my heart pounding. "Please? We're still out in public, just in case you're still doubting my intentions," he says with a playful laugh.

I grin back. "All right," I say as he leads me across the street and toward a gently weathered bench.

"You look nervous."

"I just haven't done this before," I say as I sit next to him on the bench with my hands folded in my lap, desperately trying to hide the trembling that's quickly making its way up from my toes to the tips of my fingers.

"What, visit a park?"

I smile and give him a gentle punch on his shoulder.

He pretends like it hurt. "Man, I could get use to looking at that beautiful smile of yours."

I look down at the ground. "You don't know how beautiful you are, do you?"

"What makes you say that?"

"Because every time I tell you the truth, you look down at the floor or the ground as if either of them is going to tell you something different." He moves closer to me. "But the thing is, they see what I see—a beautiful woman that took me all night to walk over to and ask if I could buy her a drink."

I hear Michael's stomach growling, bringing some levity back into the moment as we both laugh. "Maybe we should go get you something to eat."

He places his hands on his stomach. "That's embarrassing, but I'll be okay. This moment is more important to me than food. Tell me something about you. Are you a Georgia peach, as they say, or did you migrate here like most people do?"

I glance up at the sky, admiring the full moon. "I'm a Georgia peach. My mother and I lived in Marietta, but after she died when I was fourteen, I spent some time in Decatur. What about you? You don't sound like you're from here."

"I'm sorry to hear about your mother. Did you stay with family after she died?"

"My mother was the only family that I had. I never knew my father.

He died in a car accident the day I was born. I can't even tell you what he looked like because my mother never kept a picture of him anywhere in our little two-bedroom apartment. I know because I checked." I pause. "After she died, I lived on the street until I met this guy named Zee when I was eighteen. He was thirty-five." I inhale and wait for him to jump up and make a mad dash back to his car.

"I understand now why you wanted to know how old I was. It all makes sense now. So, what happened to this thirty-five-year-old guy? You stated that you were single, so I take it he's no longer in the picture."

I exhale, relieved that Michael is still here. "Zee was killed."

"I wasn't expecting that."

"Neither was I," I say without looking over at him, afraid that if I did, I would see glimmers of fear upon his face in reaction to my revelation.

"You asked where I'm from. I was born in Chicago, but my mother moved my brother and me to Georgia when I was ten, after my father left us to play in some band. The day he walked out the door, he sat me down and told me that family life wasn't for him and that he couldn't put off his dreams any longer. I then had to translate that for my brother."

"Wow."

"That's how I felt when those words dropped off his tongue so easily. It made me sick. My mother was strong. I never saw her shed a tear for him, but I'm sure when my brother and I weren't around, she cried all the time. We weren't poor, just broke. But like I said earlier, she was a waitress and worked herself to the bone to make sure we always had enough." He leans back, and even in the moonlight, I can see the depth of the grief he's trying to hide. "You know, when my brother died, I had just buried my mother a few months prior. I was just a twenty-one-year-old kid."

I reach over and place my hand on top of his.

"The intense level of pain that I experienced during that time was something that I will never forget. After I got my real estate license, I threw myself into my work and traveled some when I could. I even tried to find him. My father, that is."

"Did you?"

"I did. It wasn't hard."

"Was he still with a band?"

"That lousy joker had remarried, and his wife was pregnant with their third child."

"Sounds like the both of us have had a rough life," I say without removing my hand from his.

"Maybe that's our connection," he says as he raises my hand and places a kiss on it.

I feel my heart start thumping harder again.

"What do you mean?"

"Pain recognizes pain," he says.

I stare at him, wondering whether I'd heard him right and unsure of how to navigate a moment like this.

"What, did I say something wrong?"

"No, it's just that phrase. 'Pain recognizes pain.' It sounds like something I would say. It sounds like something I recently said."

"Well then, we think a lot alike." He gives my hand another gentle squeeze. "I haven't talked to many people about my mother or my brother. My close friend, David, encouraged me to see a shrink."

"Jack, my boss, tried to get me to do the same."

He sits up a little straighter. "And how old is this boss?"

The nervousness on his face makes me chuckle. "Jack is sixty and has been happily married for over forty years. He's more like a father to me than a boss."

I see Michael relax. "Good to hear that. I already have enough competition for your heart."

"There's no competition."

"Of course there is. I can tell I'm competing, I just don't know who or what I'm competing against. But I promise you I'm ready to get in the fight. I think you're worth it."

I glance down at the ground again.

"Mýa," he says, touching my cheek to get me to raise my eyes to him. "I meant what I said. I want to get to know you. Will you let me?"

"I'll try."

"That's all a man can ask for." His stomach begins to growl again, and I can't help but laugh hysterically. "Now, this is really embarrassing."

"Why don't we just go over to the diner and get you something to eat?"

"I will if you promise me that you'll go out with me tomorrow. We can go do something after you get off."

"I'm off tomorrow. It's my first Saturday off in two years."

"Nice. So, while you're sleeping in, I'll be wrapping up a couple of closings, but I'd love to pick you up in the evening and take you skating."

"Skating?"

"Don't tell me that you've never been skating?"

"Okay, I won't tell you that I've never been skating," I say with a smile on my face.

He claps his hands together. "This is going to be fun. I can't wait."

"What, to see me fall?"

"Don't worry; I'll bring the Vaseline. That's the perfect remedy for everything, especially falls. At least, my mother always thought so."

I feel the trembling in my knees return. "My mother used to believe that same thing—that Vaseline was the cure for everything."

The tips of his fingers are kind as he wipes away a few tears that fall down my face. "I'm glad to know that we both had the same crazy kind of mothers that loved us very much."

Chapter Eleven

—⦚⦚⦚⦚⦚—

"You're going out with a man tonight?" Jack had asked during our brief conversation earlier that next day, like he couldn't believe the impossible was finally happening. Truth be told, as Michael drives down West Ponce De Leon Avenue, I'm struggling to believe it myself.

Sitting in the passenger's seat with the window down, my arm resting on the window ledge as I listen to Michael talk about his day and take in the smell of flowers blooming and freshly cut green grass, I find that my thoughts are all over the place. I can't help but wonder if I'm feeling good because sitting here beside Michael is right, or if it just feels right because it's the first time I've been out on a real date with someone Jack would call a man. A real man.

I can hear Jack now, telling me that Zee wasn't a real man and that I should be enjoying this ride with one instead of analyzing my emotions. As Michael exits the expressway, I decide to heed Jack's imaginary advice. I close my eyes and allow the rays of the sun to rejuvenate my thoughts by focusing on the present instead of the past.

"We're almost there, just another five minutes or so," Michael says as we stop for a red light. "This place may not look like much for the outside, but you'll love it once we're inside. I can't believe you lived in Decatur and never ventured to this skating rink before. There ought to be a law against that."

His enthusiasm is refreshing.

"Is that right? A law? So this place is that serious?" I ask with a hint of sarcasm.

"It's practically historic, is all I'm saying. You'll see."

"Now I'm really looking forward to it. When I lived in Decatur, I never went anywhere. Unless you count the laundromat or the grocery store," I say.

"That's a shame. Decatur has a lot to offer. I don't get over to this side of town as much as I would like. Midtown living keeps me in a nice little bubble. I mean, everything is right there, so I don't have to go far."

"It's good that you have a car."

"I see your point," he says as we pull into a packed parking lot.

"It's busy," I say as we troll around for anything that resembles a parking spot.

"Back in the day, you'd have to park down the street and walk with your skates thrown over your shoulders. It's good to see people still appreciate art."

"Skating is art?" I ask as we finally find a spot not far from the actual building.

"Most definitely. Wait until you see what these ladies and gentlemen can do with a pair of skates. You'll come away saying the same. I promise," he says as we sit in his black BMW, admiring the way the streetlights cast a glow on the place.

"It looks more like a movie theater than a skating rink," I say.

"That's because it used to be one. I think that's why people love it. It has a much cooler vibe than other skating rinks."

"I'll have to take your word on that. How long has it been for you?" I ask.

He grins. "One thing I've noticed about you is that you have a way with questions. I think what you're really asking me is how long has it been since I brought another woman here?"

I shrug my shoulders like I have no idea what he's talking about as he steps out of the car and comes to open my door.

"I've never brought a woman here before. This place was strictly my brother's and my spot. We used to take the bus to get here on Mondays because you could rent your skates for half off. My brother was deaf, but he could feel the music's vibration in the floor. Watching him skate was amazing. You wouldn't have known he was deaf," he proudly says as I climb out of the passenger's seat, feeling foolish for asking the question in the first place.

"I'm sorry, I don't know why I asked that."

"Sure you do. You want to be sure that I'm not playing games." He stands in front of me, and I can feel the warmth of his presence on my skin. "I'm not. The moment I saw you yesterday, I knew what I wanted."

I look into his eyes, and my knees begin to wobble again. "And what do you want?" I ask as he moves even closer to me.

He leans over and whispers in my ear, "I want you."

I look down at the ground.

"There you go again." He gives me a wink, grabs my hand, and then leads me to the back of his car. "I want to show you something before we go in," he says, as he unlocks his trunk and pulls out a yellow envelope. "Here."

"What's inside?" I ask cautiously.

"Some of my work. My photography. You said that you wanted to see it last night, so I brought a few pictures for you to look at."

I open the envelope and pull out a few photos. "These are breathtaking," I say as I hold them carefully in my hands. "I love how you captured the light behind these children as they played with their pets at the park."

"I like to take photos of people with nature as a part of the action, but I'm still working on lighting."

"I can't tell, especially in this one of an older couple kissing on a bridge. It's probably my favorite."

"Mine, too. I call it *Love Endures*."

I place the photos back into the envelope and hold it out to him. "I can tell photography is your passion. Those were beautiful."

"Thank you. I'd love to get a few shots of you. I have my camera in the trunk. It would only take a few minutes."

"You don't want to photograph me."

"Why not? I love to see beauty through the lens of my camera. Besides, look up. The night sky is just coming in. Perfect timing."

I look up, and I have to agree—the sky is perfect. I know Jack would tell me to just go for it. Have some fun, he would say to me right now. "Okay."

"Great." He quickly grabs his camera bag out of the trunk and lays the envelope down inside. "I promise I'll just take a few shots."

"Why don't I believe that?"

"Because you're a smart woman."

I look around the parking lot to see if anyone is watching us.

"Don't worry; everyone is inside," he says as he checks to ensure the camera is ready.

The moment I hear him click the camera a few times to advance the film, my nerves get the best of me.

"This is silly."

"That's what makes it so unique—taking photos is all about capturing the unexpected."

"What am I supposed to do?"

"Just move. The camera and I will do the rest."

I lean against his car and look up to see the sun leaving us. I can hear the clicking of his camera, but the more I watch the way deeper hues of blue begin to take over the sky, the less I care. Every now and then, I glance at Michael. It's interesting to see how focused he is. I can feel his eyes following my every move. I feel like he's capturing my thoughts and for a second, that scares me because my thoughts are about him right now.

The way he makes me feel. The way his eyes seem to sink deep into mine. The way my knees tremble when he touches my skin. I have to keep reminding myself that this is only our first date.

But still...

"I think I got it," he finally says. "Let me just run through a few of these to be sure."

"Can I see?"

"As soon as I develop them, I'll show them to you. Deal?"

"Deal. I have to admit that it was fun. So do you develop them your-self, or do you take them somewhere?"

"I do them myself. To me, that's the best part. You get to see the light coming out of the darkness."

"Maybe you should do spoken word."

"I couldn't write if my life depended on it. I'll leave the writing and the journaling to you."

I laugh. "I didn't think I would like journaling. I'm still new at it, but I try to write a little something each night. It helps me relax."

"That's the same feeling I get when I go into my darkroom and develop the photos I've shot. I guess we have that in common, too."

"I guess we do."

He places his camera bag in the trunk and then pulls out a small plastic bag. "This is for you," he says, tossing the bag to me.

"What's this?" I ask, barely catching it.

"Are you always this cautious? Open it and see."

I slowly open the plastic bag and smile when I pull out a small jar of Vaseline.

"Something to help heal the bruises when you fall tonight."

We both can't help but laugh as he grabs my hand and we make our way inside.

—⟨⟨⟨⟨⟨•

Michael was right. The inside of the building was another world. As my eyes rove around the place, I take in a world filled with floral carpets and old hardwood floors. Bright, flashing lights and music engulfs me, makes me feel alive. I watch as people effortlessly skate around the floor. My heart skips a beat when a man does a full split, and then another does a backflip into the air.

"You were right; this is art," I say.

"I told you."

"The energy here is amazing. I love the vibe."

"I'm glad you like it. Come on, let's get our skates."

Out of the corner of my eyes, I catch a woman twirling in the center of the floor. "Wow," I say. "She moves like an ice skater."

"Close your mouth."

"I can't. I've never seen anything like this," I say as he pays for our skates and then we head toward an empty bench to put them on.

"I can't believe you've never been skating. What kinds of things did you do for fun growing up?" he asks as we slide off our shoes.

"My mother worked a lot of double shifts, but Sunday was always our day. We'd spend the whole day listening to music or playing spades."

"I haven't played spades in years. What kind of music did the two of you listen to?"

"We listened to anyone that sang jazz or blues, but my mama's favorite singer was Nina Simone," I say as I try standing in the skates.

"I've got you," he says as he stands up and wraps his arms around my waist. It's a simple touch, but feeling the strength of his hands through my white blouse is something I know I could get used to.

"I feel like I'm going to break every bone in my body with these skates on."

"If you do, I'll patch you up myself," he says, gently teasing me.

"You better take me to a real doctor," I say as I pull away from him and try to balance by myself.

Michael stands back and watches me. "It looks like you're getting the hang of this. Are you ready to go out there?"

I look at the floor filled with experienced skaters and shake my head in fear.

Michael laughs and grabs my hand. "Don't worry; I'll be right here with you. If you fall, we both fall."

"Is that a promise?"

"I won't let you go until you tell me to. That's a promise."

"Okay," I say even as the fear of falling and embarrassing myself lingers in my gut.

"You're doing great," Michael says as we make our way to the center of the rink.

"I'm okay as long as I can hold on to you," I say over the music.

"I'm glad to see that my plan is already working," he says, giving me a wink.

"Just remember that if I fall, you're going down with me."

"I'd fall for you any day."

I grin. *I might already be falling for you. Is that normal?*

"Too cheesy?" he asks as we stand in the center, watching the other skaters float effortlessly by us.

"Just a little," I say as I watch their footwork. "I think I got it. I'm going to try to stand on my own. Don't let me go too fast, now."

"I won't." He slowly removes his hand and watches as I test my balance. "That's good. The key to skating is to walk like a duck." When I glance over at him with a skeptical look on my face, he adds, "It's true. I'm not making this up."

"How am I supposed to walk like a duck?"

"It's easy. Watch me. You move forward slowly—right foot, then left foot. Slightly squat as you move. Just like a duck."

"Like this?" I ask as I gingerly try to replicate his movements.

"Yes! You're a—"

I hit the floor before he can finish his sentence.

Michael hurries to help me up. "I was just about to say that you're a natural."

"At falling? Yes, I think I have that covered very naturally."

"But at least you did it gracefully."

"Whatever. I don't see you down here."

"That's right." He allows himself to fall to the floor. "As I said, you fall, I fall."

"You did say that," I say as we enjoy a moment of laughter.

"Ready to try again?" he asks.

I glance around the skating rink, and when a five-year-old girl skates past me and laughs, I know that I need to get it together.

"Let's do this."

"That's my girl," Michael says as we stand up and then slowly move back out into the crowd.

Wait, did he just call me his girl? Ring, please.

Chapter Twelve

"How's the pizza?" Michael asks as he grabs himself a big slice of the thin crust pizza we're sharing. The edges look like they have been brushed in butter.

"It's better than I would have expected from a skating rink. It tastes homemade, to be honest."

"The owner makes the crust himself. It's probably his son doing it now, but it still tastes just as good. My mother would come here sometimes just to pick up a pie for us. Those were the best nights."

"So, you lived close to here?"

"We lived in Lithonia, but that was just the kind of mother she was."

"My mother and I never ate out. We couldn't afford it on her nurse's salary, but she was a fabulous cook. We had dozens of cookbooks. One in just about every corner of our apartment."

"I didn't realize your mother was a nurse."

"She was, and she loved it. She loved helping people."

"A good reason to become a nurse. Do you still cook?"

"I work six days a week, so I don't cook at all now, but I'd like to one day get back into it," I say, taking another bite of pizza.

"You sound like me, working that much. What was your favorite thing to cook?"

"Every Sunday, Mama and I made spaghetti and meatballs. We would make the sauce from scratch. I'm talking fresh tomatoes. I used to love rolling up the meatballs in my hands. Mama would pour her a glass of wine—the cheap kind, of course—and we would make the garlic bread. The house would smell so good that the dogs outside would start to howl. Those were the days when even the walls would smile, and life just felt right. You know what I mean?"

He reaches over the table and places his hands on mine. "I do. It's why I came here tonight. I had forgotten the good things, and I wanted to remember them again with you."

"I thought you brought me here so you could see me fall on my face?"

"That *has* been hilarious. But you're getting better, and before long, you're going to be a real pro."

"At falling, yes. I think I mentioned I have already mastered that."

"I hope you are enjoying this."

"I love it."

"That's all a man can ask for. You want this last slice of pizza?" he asks.

"No. I'm stuffed. Go for it."

"Thanks," he says, placing the last slice on his plate. "Do you cook at work?"

"Not at all. Jack does most of that, but we do have other cooks to pitch in, too. The restaurant has been in his family for years, and so have many of the recipes. People rave about his pancakes, and they should. Jack's pancakes are the lightest and fluffiest pancakes I have ever tasted. He makes a mean omelet as well."

"Jack sounds like an extraordinary man."

"He is, and his wife Mary is just the sweetest. Every Sunday, I spend pretty much the whole day with them. Mary makes spaghetti and meatballs, but it's not the same as what Mama and I used to make together. Nothing will ever taste like that again."

"It sounds like you and your mother were close, but it also sounds like Jack and Mary have an exceptional bond with you."

"They do, and I love them. After dinner, we either listen to music and dance, or if it's baseball season we'll watch the Atlanta Braves. Jack loves the Atlanta Braves."

"Well, I guess that means I won't get to take you out to dinner tomorrow," he says with a slight frown.

"I'm sorry. Our Sunday dinners have become a tradition. They would be hurt if I didn't come."

"I understand."

"Why don't you come with me?"

"You sure they wouldn't mind?"

"I'm positive."

"Great. I'll bring my apron."

"You have an apron?"

"My mother couldn't cook, so I did most of it growing up. I make a mean macaroni and cheese."

"I'm having a hard time imagining that."

"I'll have to make it for you one day."

"I'd like that," I say as I stand up, holding on to the table to balance myself.

"You leaving me already?"

"I'm going to try and make it to the restroom without killing myself or breaking a bone. I don't trust you to patch me up."

"That's a shame," he says with a flirtatious smile. "Use the wall to keep yourself upright."

"Good idea."

By the time I make my way back, the lights are dim, but I spot Michael standing at the entrance of the skating rink floor.

"You ready to get back out there?" he asks as I carefully stop in front of him.

"Sure." I take his hand, and we move back onto the floor.

"You are doing much better. I still believe that by the end of the night, you'll be skating around here like a pro."

"A girl in the restroom had mercy on me and gave me a few pointers."

Just as we take our first turn, I hear Nina Simone singing "My Baby Just Cares for Me."

"I love this song."

"I was counting on that."

"You had them play this song for me?"

"I had them play it for *us*."

Can this night get any better?

He moves slowly in front of me and places his hands on my waist again. "I'm going to skate backward so you can stay skating forward. Just stay close to me. I won't let you fall."

Yes, it can.

I nod and wrap my arms around his neck, allowing him to guide me around the floor.

So this is what a real man feels like?

Chapter Thirteen

—⁂⁂⁂—

"R elax," Jack says as he watches me pace back and forth. "You've been a nervous wreck all day, kid."

"Maybe I shouldn't have invited him."

Jack gets up from his gray cloth chair and grabs my hands. "Tonight will be great. Listen. Do you hear that? That's Mary in the kitchen fixing her best pot of spaghetti and meatballs for your man."

"*My man*. That sounds so strange, Jack."

"But I bet it rolls off your tongue nicely," he says. I smile as I glance down at my watch for the hundredth time. Jack squeezes my hands. "I've never seen you this excited; I like it."

I sink down onto their gray sofa and glance at my watch again as Jack takes a seat next to me.

"What's really wrong, kid?"

"I'm going to have to tell him," I say with a sigh. "About my past."

"Why would you do that? I mean, what's left to tell him? He knows you lived on the streets, and you told him about how you dated a thirty-five-year-old man when you were only a kid, and he's still coming tonight for dinner. I'd say he knows exactly what he needs to know."

"Jack."

I watch as his face softens into what I think of as a fatherly expression, and I know a lecture is coming.

"You remember what I told you about a woman's closet?"

"I do."

"Well, now you have more clothes in your closet, that's all. Let the past stay buried under them. Michael doesn't need to know about the five years you were away. That part of your story is done. Even if Michael were to look you up, he wouldn't find anything. I have your background check, so

I know it's clean. You've got nothing to worry about, so just enjoy this. Enjoy having a man fight for your heart." Jack stands up. "You deserve this, kid."

Mary walks into the living room as the doorbell rings.

"It's him," I say.

"Well, go answer the door before the heat melts him," Jack says with a grin.

"How do I look?" I ask, adjusting my skirt as I make my way to the door.

"You look like a beautiful woman about to open the front door," Mary says with a quick nod of approval.

I adjust my skirt once more and then take a deep breath. "Here goes," I say as I open the door and see Michael standing there with an apron in one hand and a bottle of wine in the other. My eyes take in his dark jeans, white collared shirt, and black sport coat. "You look handsome."

"Thank you. I'm ready to cook."

"I see. I thought you were kidding when you said you were going to bring your apron," I say, staring at him like some giddy teenager rather than a grown woman of twenty-seven years.

"For the record, you look great, too. And you smell good," he says as he moves inside.

"It's not me that smells good—it's the food."

Michael leans over and kisses me on the cheek. "Yes, the food smells good, but you smell even better," he whispers as I lead him into the living room.

"Hi, I'm Mary. It's so good to meet Mýa's boyfriend." I try to hide how much I'm blushing, but Michael, of course, is all smiles as Mary takes the bottle of wine from him and adds, "Mýa wasn't lying when she said how handsome you were."

Michael looks over at me, and I, of course, pretend like I have never said such a thing to her. Jack is quiet, but I see him giving Michael a good once-over, and even smiling as he takes notice of Michael's hard-bottom shoes.

"You must be Jack," Michael says, extending his hand.

"I am."

"Mýa speaks very highly of you and Mary."

"That's always nice to hear," Jack says, giving me a quick nod of approval.

"You have a lovely home. I love red brick homes; they are hard to find."

"Mary and I brought this old, two-story home right after we were married. Mary loves how quiet this neighborhood is. I like it because it's close to the restaurant."

"Well, you two have certainly kept it up. The matching red brick staircase that leads up to the black door is a nice touch." Michael says. Jack just stares at him for a moment. "Sorry, when you're a real estate agent, you tend to notice things like that."

Jack's face relaxes. "Right. I forgot you're a real estate agent. Well, this house needs a little work now, but Mary and I do our best with it. Mary here keeps trying to get me to change the color of the walls in this room. She thinks we should go from cream to off-white, but frankly, I'm not convinced there's a difference between the two."

Michael looks over at me, and I shake my head as a warning not to get in the middle of that debate. He nods and then reaches in his back pocket and pulls out a white envelope.

"These are for you."

We all watch Jack slowly open the envelope and pull out two tickets. "Look, Mary! It's a pair of tickets to see the Braves next Sunday. We're going to the game!" He glances down at the tickets again. "These are great seats! We're going in style. Mary, get your good dress out!"

Mary comes over and inspects the tickets. "I'm not pulling out a dress for a baseball game, but I will go and buy me a pair of those fancy Jordache jeans all the girls are wearing these days," she says with a chuckle. "Thank you so much, Michael. Jack has never been to a Braves game. You just made our day."

"No, he made my life!"

"I thought I was your life," Mary says with a playful frown.

"You are and always will be, little lady," Jack says as he leans over and places a kiss on Mary's cheek.

I mouth a thank you to Michael as Jack and Mary continue to look at their tickets.

"I'm hungry," I say to get their attention.

Jack places the tickets in his pocket and Mary beckons to us, leading the way to the table as she says, "Right, let's eat."

As I take my seat, questions continue to play in my mind. Is Jack right? Is Michael *my man?*

When Michael places his hand on top of mine, and Mary places the bread on the table just as Jack begins to tell jokes about all the mistakes I made when I first started at the restaurant, I know the answer.

I know the answer with all my heart.

Chapter Fourteen

—⟨⟨⟨⟨⟨•

"**M**ary, that was outstanding," Jack says as he rubs his distended stomach. "We should have company over more often."

"Hey, I'm company," I say with a pout.

"You're not company, kid. You're our daughter, so you don't count."

"You're right, and I wouldn't have it any other way," I say as Jack reaches over and gives my hand a gentle squeeze.

Mary chimes in as she starts gathering the empty dishes. "Jack's right; daughters don't count." She glances over at Michael and gives him a playful wink. "I'm sure you can tell she got her beautiful looks from me, can't you, Michael?"

"Of course. Mýa certainly doesn't look like Jack."

The laughter around the table is perfect. It reminds me of the laughter Mama and I used to share as we cleaned up the mess we always made in the kitchen.

"Let me help you with those, Mary," I say, standing up.

"Child, sit back down," she says, pointing to my chair. "Jack, go put on some music. I'm just going to throw these dishes in the sink, and when I come back, we can get the dancing going."

Jack stands up. "I've got an even better idea. Why don't we just leave the dishes here for a while and move to the living room so we can listen to Mýa sing?"

Michael looks over at me as I glare at Jack. "You sing?"

"She sure does," Jack replies for me, ignoring my thunderous look.

"And she has a beautiful voice," Mary says with a slight chuckle as she catches sight of my facial expression.

"I can't wait to hear this," Michael says, standing up eagerly.

"Our company has spoken. Let's go," Jacks happily exclaims.

My knees begin to wobble as we head toward the living room.

"Mýa, why don't you stand in the center? And Michael, you can have a seat on the sofa."

"Okay, what should I sing?" I ask, locking my knees together to keep them from buckling underneath me.

"'Feeling Good,' of course," Jack says, flashing me a victorious smile. I return it with a smirk that promises we'll talk about this later, but he ignores that, too, as he and Mary take their seats.

"Wait," Mary says, jumping back up. "Let me get each of us a little wine. We still have some left from the bottle that Michael brought."

"Hurry up."

Mary shoots Jack a disapproving look.

"Hurry up, *dear*, I meant."

"I'll take it," Mary says, smiling as she hurries into the kitchen.

"Barely got myself out of that one," Jack says, wiping his forehead.

Michael lets out a laugh as I stand there, knees still wobbling, throat feeling dry, and trying not to lose what little bit of bravery I have mustered up.

I can feel Michael's eyes on me, but I refuse to look his way.

"I'm back," Mary says, walking into the living room carrying four glasses of wine on a silver platter. "There wasn't enough wine left in the bottle that Michael brought us, so I opened a new one."

I grab my glass and gulp it down quickly, making Jack chuckle.

"Okay, kid, now that you've got a little liquid courage in you, let's hear some Nina Simone," he says as Mary takes my glass away.

Just breathe. He's just a man. My man, and a really handsome man. A really handsome man that—girl, sing.

I close my eyes and think about yesterday, and the moment that came into existence as Michael photographed me in the parking lot of the skating rink. My thoughts focus on how his eyes watched me as I moved under the setting of the sun. My skin relives the intimacy that we shared with only a camera between us. My heart reminds me that I've never had a man capture it with the click of a device. I wondered what he will see when he stands in his darkroom, waiting for my face to appear as he slowly moves the film back and forth under the development mixture.

What will a piece of film tell him about me?

What will it show?

Will it show him the loneliness that he's slowly taking away from the core of my soul?

Will it show him the laughter that he's giving to my lungs?

Or the taste that he makes my lips crave?

As I dig deeper into the lyrics of the song, I can feel the weight of my fear in the palms of my hands.

Am I finally ready to let go?

Am I finally ready to be free of my fear that no one could love… someone like me?

Chapter Fifteen

A s I walk Michael to the door, I notice the smile that graced his face most of the night has now been replaced by a more serious look. He seems distant, lost in thought.

"What's wrong?" I ask.

"Can we go for a walk?"

"Sure."

I tell myself not to worry as we make our way down the stairs and onto the sidewalk, but I can't help but feel like maybe he thinks it was too soon for him to meet my "parents."

The silence in the night air hovers around us as Jack and Mary's house begins to fade into the scenery behind us.

"I see why Mary likes this neighborhood. It is very quiet. You don't even hear any dogs barking," Michael says, grabbing my hand as we walk down the street.

"What's wrong, Michael?" I ask again, unable to stand the suspense any longer.

He stops and pulls me close to him. "I didn't want to say this in front of everyone."

I pull back, afraid he's about to end something that my heart feels could last forever. "This was too soon, wasn't it? Meeting Jack and Mary, I mean."

He gently pulls me back to him and allows the tips of his fingers to rest on my waist. "It wasn't too soon. I enjoyed meeting both of them. Actually, I'm glad we've gotten that out of the way."

"Then, what is it?" I ask while searching his eyes for something that will ease my nerves.

"I want to be your man, Mýa. I know that sounds old-fashioned, but I think it's best to just put it out there so there isn't any doubt about exclusivity moving forward. Are you okay with that?"

The pace of my heartbeat slows down as I reach out and touch his cheek. "I want that, too."

His fingers move upward until they find a resting place on the back of my neck. "I can feel you trembling."

"It's a good thing," I say as his lips come closer, shortening the space between us.

"I'm going to kiss you now."

"That's a good thing, too," I say just before his lips reach mine.

While this isn't my first kiss, it's the first kiss that has me wanting more. More happiness. More joy. Even more love, perhaps.

"Man, I'm glad we got that out of the way," Michael says as we stand there holding each other, allowing our hearts time to come back from that place that hearts go when they want to connect in a space where no one else exists. "I've been wanting to kiss you since that night in the park."

"You make it sound like that wasn't just a couple of days ago."

"When you want to kiss someone as badly as I did, two days seems like an eternity," he says as we begin to make our way back to Jack and Mary's house.

"I didn't realize how far we walked," I say as I take a quick look back.

Michael wraps his hand around mine again. "You know, when you were singing that song, I wanted to jump up and kiss you then. I'm going to have that song in my head all night. Your voice was mesmerizing. Who knew you could blow like that?"

His words bring a smile to my face, although I can't say that I agree with them. Singing is one thing. Being able to "blow" is something quite different.

Nina can blow. Billie can blow.

"I can't 'blow,' as you put it," I say.

"Yes, you can, and you did. You need to do something with that," he says as we finally reach Jack and Mary's block.

"Like what?"

"I don't know, but it definitely should involve you going into a recording studio or singing at one of these jazz restaurants."

"You sound like Jack."

"Jack is a smart man."

"I've never considered it. Not sure if singing is something I want to do."

"You can't wait tables for the rest of your life. Not that I'm saying anything is wrong with that, but with a voice like that, waiting tables should not be a forever kind of thing."

"I was thinking about getting my real estate license."

"Okay, now you're messing with me. I'm serious, Mýa."

"I don't know if I could leave Jack."

"The Jack I met would want you to leave if that meant pursuing singing as a career. He wants something more for you. I could tell by the way he was pushing you to sing tonight."

"Jack wants me to get married."

"What father doesn't? But I'm sure he wants you to marry a man who can support your passion, and you can't convince me that delivering a tall stack of pancakes with a side of bacon does that."

I stop and let his words roll around in my head, unsure if I'm ready to do anything with them just yet. "I don't know if singing is right for me. For me, singing has always been this 'thing' that I can do. I doubt anyone besides you, Jack, and Mary would want to hear me sing in a professional manner."

"I think you're scared of putting yourself out there. And that's understandable. Letting the world see inside you is a scary thing."

"Maybe," I say as we begin walking again.

"Atlanta has an array of jazz restaurants that I know would be interested. At least give it a try."

"I'll think about it."

"That's all a man can ask for," he says as we reach Jack and Mary's house.

Chapter Sixteen

"**M**orning, Jack," I sing as I walk into the restaurant around five-thirty the next morning. Jack comes from around the counter with his apron covered in pancake mix, bacon grease, and spilled coffee. "Your apron looks like we've opened and closed already."

"Someone is in a good mood today," he says, giving me a once-over. "I wonder why?"

I try not to blush. "Whatever."

"Don't 'whatever' me. I've never seen you come in here with that much pep in your step. Maybe you feel so good that you could pull a double shift?"

Just like that, my singing stops. "Jack."

"Sorry, kid. Misty isn't coming in for the afternoon shift, and you know how crazy Monday lunch can be."

"Okay," I say with a sigh. "Good thing we're only open for breakfast and lunch. Michael and I are going to the movies tonight."

I can't help but grin at the thought of being with Michael again. I glance down at my arm. *Are those goosebumps?*

Jack is staring at me when I look up. "What?"

"You're still mad at me for making you sing in front of Michael last night, aren't you?" he asks.

"I'm not mad," I say as I walk back to the kitchen to get my breakfast, knowing he will follow.

"Good, because if your singing doesn't make him fall in love with you, I don't know what will."

"Jack, it's too early to be talking about love," I say, grabbing a couple of pancakes and tossing them on my plate.

"Please. I knew I was in love with Mary after six dates. I just didn't tell her for a couple of months."

I pour myself a cup of coffee and take a seat. "Why not?"

Jack takes a seat as well. "I don't know, really. I guess I didn't want to scare her off, and maybe I was afraid she didn't feel the same way about me."

"Did she? When you finally told her, did she feel the same way?"

The smile on Jack's face tells me that he's thinking about that moment—that moment when everything was finally right in his world.

"I'll never forget that day. There my Mary sat under a tree, reading a book. You should have seen the way the sun fell on her, causing her beautiful brown skin to glow and her eyes to sparkle like diamonds. The sight of her made me want to throw caution to the wind and tell her how I felt."

"How did you do it? How did you tell her?"

"It wasn't anything fancy, but it changed my whole life. I walked over and sat down next to her, took her book and set it off to the side, and then I just let the words flow. I wish you could have seen how she smiled at me, but it was what she said that felt even better in my heart. Mary told me that she loved me as much as I loved her. That was new to me. To get that kind of love returned—well, it's a blessing. You know I'm not a religious man, but I give thanks for that day. We were married a month later. It was a simple wedding, but neither of us wanted anything beyond that. We already had everything we needed in each other."

As Jack places his hand on his heart, I feel tears well up in the corners of my eyes. "I hope to have a moment like that one day," I finally say.

"You will. That I can promise."

"How can you be so sure?"

"I saw it in that young man's eyes last night. I think he will beat my timing of six dates."

"Men aren't the same as they were back in your day, Jack."

He taps the table. "You're probably right about that, but I'm right about Michael."

I try to act like I'm not buying it as I sip my coffee, but my heart is pleading for it to be so.

"You like him, too. That's why you came in here singing this morning."

"I wasn't singing."

"Sure, and I didn't spill coffee on myself."

"Don't forget the pancake mix and bacon grease."

"My point exactly."

I laugh as I get up and put on my name tag.

"You two going out tonight?"

I gather my plate and coffee cup in my hands. "You don't remember? I mentioned earlier that we're going to the movies."

"That's right."

"I am so excited. I haven't been to the movies since I was a little girl. Mama and I would go when they had the two-dollar movie special on Tuesdays."

"Those were the days," Jack says wistfully. "I remember when going to the movies cost a quarter, but a couple of dollars isn't bad. I bet that in the six months you were with Zee, he never spent two dollars to take you to see a movie."

"Jack, you're a mess."

"Mary tells me that all the time."

I walk over to the sink and put my plate and coffee cup down inside. I can feel Jack's eyes following me.

"Jack," I say slowly as I turn toward him. "I'm going to tell you something, but I don't want you to get too excited."

"I can't make that promise, kid, until I hear what you've got to say."

"Fair enough," I say, although I know he's going to get all worked up anyway. "Michael and I were talking last night, and he thinks that I should see if one of these jazz restaurants is looking for a singer." I watch as Jack's face lights up. "Now Jack, remember what I just said. Don't go getting all excited just yet. I told Michael that I would think about it."

"What's there to think about? Mary and I would be happy to take you to each audition when the time comes. Which I know will be soon if you just go for it."

"I'm not sure I want to put that kind of pressure on myself—or put myself out there, for that matter."

"Look, kid, life is about putting yourself out there. I wouldn't be where I am today if I hadn't done exactly that when my Mary came along. You can't stop the bad stuff from happening by putting yourself in a bubble. And staying in a bubble keeps the good stuff from getting in as well. In life, you take the good with the bad and you make lemonade. That voice of yours is a pitcher that wasn't designed to just sit in a cabinet and look pretty. It was made to help you serve up that lemonade."

I walk over and hug him. "You truly are amazing, Jack. I don't know where or how you come up with your illustrations, but I love you so much for sharing them with me."

"I love you, too, kid, but enough of this hugging stuff," Jack says while acting like he's wiping my hug off his shirt. "I can't have everyone here thinking they can get a hug off this old man as well."

"Then I would get jealous," Mary says as she walks in. "Why does everyone want to hug my man?"

"No one wants to hug me except you, dear."

Mary gives Jack the side-eye, so he blows a kiss at her.

"Mýa was just telling me that Michael is going to help her find out if one of these jazz restaurants is looking for a singer."

"I said that I would think about it, remember?"

"I thought you said that you loved my illustration of the pitcher?"

"I did, but I'm not sure if I'm ready to pull that pitcher out of the cabinet just yet."

"I think you should at least see if any opportunities exist out there," Mary says as she moves next to Jack, the two of them presenting a united front.

I try not to laugh at the picture they make. "Are you two ganging up on me?" I ask, placing my hands on my hips.

"Of course not. Think of this as giving you the push that you need," Mary says in a motherly tone.

"What happens if I find something and they want to hire me? I don't think I could ever leave here."

"Mýa, you've got too much talent for this old pancake house. As soon as you land a job as a singer, you're fired. I mean that!"

"Jack, you aren't really going to fire me, are you?"

"The very day the ink is dry, you're out of here," Jack says with a stern look on his face.

I look at Mary, who is nodding her head in agreement. "But I love working here with you and Mary."

"Mýa, honey, what Jack is saying is that we want something better for you. Right, Jack?"

"You can put it to her however you want. I said what I said, and I meant what I said."

I have never seen Jack so determined, but I know that his firmness is coming from the right place, so I decide not to argue about the subject any longer. "Okay, Jack. If I find something, I'll quit. But for the record, it has to pay me way more than what I make here."

"That shouldn't be hard," Mary says.

Jack gives her a stern look, but Mary blows him a playful kiss. I grin as I watch the two of them.

"Let's get to work so our Mýa here doesn't have to wear an apron for the rest of her life," Jack says, clapping his hands together.

Mary and I can't help but laugh as he opens up the front doors like he's in a hurry all of a sudden.

Chapter Seventeen

I'm plumb tired as I glance at the clock and see that it's almost seven. The Goodwill bag that holds my outfit for the evening—a cute little black and pink summer dress with thick shoulder straps—is still where I threw it the moment I walked in the door of my apartment.

I need some motivation to get myself moving, so I put a Minnie Riperton record on and allow the words of "Loving You" to breathe new energy into my bones as I head to the shower.

Four songs later, my head is still bobbing as I slip on my dress and slide into a pair of black flats. I slap a little water and mousse in my hair to give it some curl action, and then quickly dab on some gold glitter eye shadow. Checking myself out in the mirror, I feel a little overdressed for a movie. But time isn't on my side, and neither is a pair of clean jeans.

Michael knocks at the door, and I immediately wish I had washed the load of laundry neatly piled in the corner of my bedroom like I was supposed to over the weekend. Let Jack tell it, I was too busy having a boyfriend and falling in love.

Is Jack right? Can I see Love Lane just up ahead?

I inhale deeply and then open the door. "Hi, there. Sorry to keep you waiting."

"You look great. But is everything okay? You seem a little winded."

"Sorry, I found myself rushing there at the end," I say, admiring his tailored black pants, white collared shirt, and black tie. "You look nice."

"Here, let me help you catch your breath," he says, sweeping me into his arms and placing a kiss on my lips.

"That kiss didn't help," I say as I struggle to gain my composure.

"Just trying to do my part."

"I'm sure."

"I can always try again."

He moves to pull me close again, but I hold out my hand. "We don't have time for that if we're going to make it on time." I see the disappointment on his face and smile. "Do you think this dress is too much for a movie?"

"I like it, but why don't we get dinner instead of a movie? That way, you won't feel overdressed, and I won't feel bad that I didn't get a chance to change out of this shirt and tie before heading over here."

"I like the shirt and tie."

"Then I'm glad I had to keep them on." He steps over the threshold, and I realize that it's the first time he's seen my barely furnished apartment. I follow his eyes as they move around my small space. "We always meet downstairs, but it's nice to see that you live on the basics just like me."

"I know it's not much."

"It's more than I had when I rented my first apartment, trust me," he says as I grab my purse.

I love how he seems to know how to make me feel better, make me feel like I'm normal. "One day, I'm going to buy a sofa and put some paint on the walls," I say, closing the door behind us.

"Yeah, I told myself that, too, when I moved into my place in Midtown. Hasn't happened yet."

The light laughter that fills the air between us feels so natural. As we walk toward Michael's car, I look up and see that the stars are enjoying the picture of us just as much as I am.

"Why don't we stop at Marco's first and then get dinner?" Michael suggests as he opens my car door.

"I didn't realize they were open during the week," I say as I slide in.

"They are. At least, that's what my buddy David told me," Michael says as he starts the car up.

"He and his wife just had a baby, right?"

"A boy. They named him Justin Montgomery Myers."

"He sounds important already."

"Doesn't he?"

"I know they can't be more excited."

"David is on me because I haven't had the chance to see him yet. But I reminded him that Michelle and the baby just came home yesterday, and I wanted to give them all some bonding time before I took over his love, being the uncle and all."

I laugh. "Why don't we go together?"

"Are you serious? That would be great. I'll call David as soon as I can and make the arrangements. He and Michelle have been eager to meet you, too, so that would be perfect."

As I look out the window, I see my life flashing by. I see myself smiling. I see myself happy. Things that I have never seen as possibilities before are now as clear as the stoplights that we encounter. And I have to admit that it all scares me.

Does someone like me deserve to be this happy?

"You okay over there?" Michael's voice breaks into my reverie. "You aren't nervous about meeting David and Michelle, are you? Don't be. They are both the most down-to-earth people I know, and they're probably the closest thing to family that I have."

I lean my head back against my seat. "It's not that," I say, briefly glancing over at him.

"Okay, then tell me what's got you staring out that window with such seriousness."

"This is just strange, that's all. I mean, for the last four years, it's been just me. Well, me, Jack and Mary."

"You never dated anyone after that thirty-five-year-old?"

"Don't say it like that," I say, tapping him jokingly on the shoulder.

"Okay, let me rephrase that. You never dated anyone else before working for Jack?"

"After that thirty-five-year-old died, I was…I was…unavailable."

"Emotionally?"

"In every way, really."

"So, you really loved him?"

"He helped me get out of a very dark period in my life."

"You mean when you lived on the street after your mother died?"

"Yeah."

"But did you love him?"

"I was eighteen. What eighteen-year-old really knows what love is? Well, I take that back. Jack was eighteen when he met Mary, and he swears that he fell in love with her after only six dates."

"You don't think that's possible?" he asks.

"You sound like you do."

"Some people don't believe in love at first sight. Some people believe do. As for me, I believe that when it comes to love—real love—anything is possible."

I scoot over and place my head on his shoulder.

"Your hair smells nice."

"It's the mousse."

"Then I love the mousse."

Was that his way of saying that he's already on Love Lane?

Chapter Eighteen

"It's not packed tonight," I say as the hostess leads Michael and I to a table by the stage.

"It's still a good crowd, and the band is playing some good music," Michael says as we take our seats.

"I wonder if they do spoken word during the week?" I ask after we've placed our drink order.

"I believe it's open mic tonight, so anyone can perform."

"Nice. That means that we'll get to hear some of the locals," I say as the waitress places our drinks on the table and I take a quick survey of the crowd and notice that most of them have on business attire. "There are a lot of shirts and ties tonight."

Michael glances around the room. "I'm sure people come here after work for happy hour. This is Midtown, after all."

I nod as a gregarious man with a brown short-brimmed hat, smooth chocolate skin, and wide set eyes steps up on the stage.

"Is there a Mýa in the audience tonight?" he asks.

Michael's hand shoots up in the air, and he begins pointing at me directly over my head to get the announcer's attention.

What in the world? Why is he pointing at me and how does that man on the stage know my name?

"What's going on?" I ask nervously.

"Ladies and gentlemen, it's come to our attention that this beautiful lady can blow. So, we need all of you out there to clap until she agrees to come up here and show us how it's done. Rumor has it that she might be shy."

The audience doesn't hesitate to comply. As the clapping starts to pick up speed, I shoot Michael an annoyed look, but he keeps his eyes on the stage.

He must have already learned from Jack how to ignore my looks.

"Okay, she's not moving, so that means that we all have to clap harder."

Again, the audience doesn't hesitate to comply, and neither does Michael as he joins in.

When the pressure of it all finally gets to me, I stand up and slowly make my way to the stage.

"What are you going to sing for us tonight?" the announcer asks when I'm standing next to him.

Oh my. I glance over at Michael. *I can't believe this is really happening. I'm going to kill that man of mine. What in the world am I suppose to sing?*

"How about Billie Holiday?" I ask as I turn my attention back to the announcer. "I can sing 'Our Love Is Here to Stay.'"

"Great choice. I'll let you get to it," the announcer says, and then makes his way off the stage.

I clear my throat as the lights dim, pray my nerves will behave themselves, and wrap my fingers around the microphone. A few seconds later, the saxophonist leads me in, and the melody he belts out overpowers me, overpowers my nerves and even my moment of anger over being put on the spot like this.

By the time the drums chime in, I feel like I'm fourteen years old again, standing in front of Mama. I can see her holding a glass of wine in her hand, as she often did on Sunday nights. "Sing for me, baby," she would urge. "Let me hear that beautiful voice that takes all my sorrow away."

I would wait for Mama to close her eyes and then I would open my mouth and allow the lyrics to surge out of me like they were on a mission—a mission to drive away everything that pained her. It was a pain that she never spoke about, but one I could always feel hidden under the tears that she never wanted me to see her shed.

Tears that her Vaseline couldn't wipe away, pain that it couldn't heal.

I often wondered if the pain and the tears were because of him—the father that I never knew. Did she love him so much that the pain of losing him made it impossible to utter his name? Or did he hurt her so bad that the thought of him did the same? I imagine it was both. It had to be.

Will I experience the same heartbreak?

Opening my eyes after I end the song, tears sting my eyes and beg me to let them fall. But as I look over at Michael and hear the applause from the crowd, the lights come back on and I'm thankful that for once, I don't feel the need to honor their request.

"Ladies and gentlemen, her boyfriend was right. This little lady can blow!" the announcer says.

Chapter Nineteen

"I'm going to kill you for that," I say as I sit back down and use my napkin to dab the corners of my eyes.

"It wasn't meant to make you cry. I'm so sorry," Michael says as he hands me his napkin, too.

I see the genuine concern on his face and quickly reassure him as I place my napkin back on the table. "It's not you. I don't know why, but for some reason, that song reminded me of when I used to sing for my mother."

"I wish I could have met her. I bet she was as beautiful as you are."

"She was beautiful. Her smile was infectious."

"So that's where you get it from."

I can feel myself blushing. *There he goes again, making me feel better.* "So, you had this all planned? There was no going to the movies?" I ask as I take a sip of my now watered-down martini.

"Guilty, but know that I lied out of the sincerity of my heart," Michael says while trying to look as innocent as possible.

"Sincerity of your heart, huh?"

"Look, you needed to know how good you really are. That way, you'd feel more comfortable and confident when the time came to step into a studio or to sing more than one song on a stage. I figured the best way to do that was to let people who had no connection to you tell you so."

"An unbiased option: that's what this was?" I ask, amused at how well-thought-out his plan was and secretly loving the fact that he did it all for me.

"Did it work?"

I lean back slightly in my chair and look around, avoiding his eye. "Yeah, it worked."

"That's all a man can ask for," Michael says with a chuckle as the announcer comes over to our table and pulls up a chair.

"Hey, I'm Marco," he says as he holds out his hand for me to shake.

I take it, glancing at Michael and wondering if this was something else that he planned. If he had anything to do with it, nothing in his expression gives him away.

"I'll get straight to why I came over," Marco says as he pulls his chair closer to the table. "The band needs a female voice, and after what I heard tonight, I think you would be a perfect fit."

"I already have a job."

"Yeah, your boyfriend told me that you were a waitress when he called. That can't be getting it done," Marco says matter-of-factly. "With a voice like that, you deserve to be making more. I'm talking real dollars each week."

"How much more?" Michael asks.

"What, you're her manager now?"

"Just looking out for her best interest, that's all," Michael quickly says.

I continue to sit there quietly, trying to get a grasp on what is happening and why.

"I get it. If Mýa here were my lady, I'd do the same. But don't worry, every member in that band up there will tell you that I'm fair and that I'm not looking to take advantage of anyone. I want the American dream—a thriving business—and I know we can make that happen. Her voice will keep the tables packed," Marcos says enthusiastically as he turns his attention back to me. "Not that we're not doing good now. You feel me? But with you, we could take this thing to a whole new level. That means everyone will be making money. You get where I'm coming from?"

"I understand," I say.

"Proper little thing. I like it. But in all seriousness, I see this as a win-win for each of us."

"You still didn't tell her how much you are offering," Michael says as he leans over the table and takes my hand in his. "You need to give her something to think about."

Marco nods his head in agreement. "A businessman after my own heart. Okay. Here's the scoop. I'll pay you three hundred a night. That's nine hundred a week to perform weekends only—Friday through Sunday. Plus, you'll get some of the band's tips. That could easily be another hundred or two. So, now we're talking $3,600 or more in your pocket each month. I know you're not pulling that kind of money as a waitress. Am I right?"

My knees are knocking under the table as I consider how that kind of money could help me get a car and a new place—no more riding the bus or looking at the peeling walls of my apartment. I have to admit, it all sounds so good, but how could I leave Jack?

"I'll think about it," I say as I take another sip of my martini. "I can't make any promises right now."

I don't miss the shocked look on Marco's face, even though he's trying hard not to show it. "That's cool, but don't think too long. I'm ready to get this thing going," he says as he stands up. "You should thank your boyfriend for talking me into letting you sing tonight. I'm not going to lie, I'm glad I listened."

"You want to go by the park and talk?" Michael asks as Marco takes the stage again and thanks the crowd.

I nod and grab my purse, glancing up at the stage once more. A couple of the band members give me a quick wave. I wave back. *Wait, what are you doing?*

Michael smiles. "Look at you, already making friends."

"Whatever," I say, giving Michael a playful little shove toward the door. "Let's go."

Out the corner of my eye, I see Marco watching us.

Chapter Twenty

"You have to love these hot summer nights in Georgia," Michael says, removing his tie as we take a seat on the weathered gray bench.

"It is hot, but I still love how peaceful the night air is. You can hear the bees humming in the trees behind us. They have a purpose, and they know what that purpose is," I say.

"You feel like your purpose is to be there for Jack?"

I shrug my shoulders. "Maybe, but Jack wouldn't agree with me."

"That's because he wants something better for you."

"I know, but I'm not sure Marco's is it. Don't get me wrong, the money would allow me to finally get a car and even a better place. But there's something about Marco that just doesn't sit right with me."

"Like what?"

"I don't know how to explain it, but it was the way he spoke; it reminded me of someone else."

"Your thirty-five-year-old love?"

"Yes, but not in the way that you're probably imagining."

Michael places his arm around me, and I find comfort in resting my head on his shoulder. "I understand."

"You're not disappointed?" I ask, raising my head so I can search his face.

"There are other places that you could sing at. They might not pay as much; then again, they could pay more. The important thing is for you to feel comfortable," he says, placing a kiss on my forehead. "Do you want me to call around?"

"I will," I say, surprising myself with the sincerity in my voice.

"Wow, I wasn't expecting to hear that, but I'm glad that you said it. Why the change?"

"Tonight, the memories of singing in front of my mother made me cry a little, but it also made me feel something that I haven't felt since I was a little girl full of romantic notions."

"Romantic notions?"

"Stop. I'm serious."

"Sorry, but can we come back to those romantic notions after you've finished your serious thought?"

I roll my eyes at him and give him a wry smile. "Like I was *saying*, it felt like something was opening up."

"Like what?"

"The future and all the possibilities that come with it."

"I see that as a good thing. A reason why *we* should continue to pursue this."

"We?" I ask, glancing up at him and immediately falling deep into his eyes.

"As Marco said, I'm your boyfriend."

"I'm not sure I've ever really had one of those."

"What about what's-his-name? Oh yes, Zee."

"Jack would say that he doesn't count."

"That's great news for me."

"And why is that great news for you?" I ask, playing into the lightness of the shift in mood.

"Because that means that I'm your first, and I hope to be your last."

My last?

"Do you really mean that? All of that? Including the part about being my last?"

He tilts my chin up and places his warm summer lips upon mine, making me feel like a little girl dancing on the top of soft clouds.

"Does that answer your question?"

"I'm not sure," I say. "I think I need some more convincing."

When he pulls me close enough to feel his heart beating against my own chest, I don't stop at just turning onto Love Lane. I'm flying down it with my head hanging out the window, screaming joyfully. *This is what love should feel like.*

Chapter Twenty-one

T his is going worse than I thought it would.

I watch Jack pace the floor in front of me, hands in the air, and he stops a few times to point at me in heated anger.

"I can't believe you're going to turn him down!" Jack says, outraged with my decision not to go with Marco's offer. "Am I going to have to fire you so you can go live the life that you need to be living?"

"Jack, let me explain," I say, trying to defuse the situation, but Jack isn't listening.

He looks at Mary. "Say something to her, because I just can't right now."

"Sweetie, think about what you could accomplish by making that kind of money. Think about how much better your life would be," Mary quickly says as she reaches over and places a concerned hand on my shoulder.

I look at each of them, my heart melting as I see the love they have for me. It reminds me of Mama.

"Can we all just go talk in the office?" I plead as I look around and notice that everyone has stopped working because they are deeply engrossed in our conversation.

Mary grabs Jack by the hand and leads him to the office as he continues his rant about how unreasonable I'm being, heedless of who's listening. I follow closely behind and hope Jack will give me a chance to explain before he actually fires me.

I close the door and lean against the wall as Jack plops down in his chair, still huffing and puffing. Mary takes a seat and tries to calm him down, but it wasn't working.

"All right, kid, we're away from listening ears. Now, explain yourself," Jack demands.

I glance over at the statue and then move a little closer to Jack's desk as I murmur, "Marco reminded me of Zee." Jack drops his shoulders, so I go on. "It was the way he spoke. I felt like he was trying to convince me to do something, and not in a good kind of way. I could hear the manipulation in his voice. It was so familiar. The moment Michael and I left, I understood why I felt that way. It was the same feeling I had that night with Zee—the night that forever put blood in my memories."

Mary stands up and comes over to hug me. "I'm so sorry, Mýa. Jack and I should have known there was more to this. I'm sorry we didn't give you a chance to explain first."

I see the sadness in Jack's eyes and give them a small smile as I say, "It's okay, Mary. I know you both love me."

"We really do," Mary says softly as tears begin to gather in her eyes.

"I am going to sing," I say, looking in Jack's direction again. "I'm not giving up on that. It just won't be at Marco's."

Jack sits up in his chair and I smile as his bowed head lifts up.

"That's wonderful, honey! Something else is going to come along. Just you wait and see. I bet it will even pay more," Mary says.

"Thank you. I'm finally realizing that I want this. Last night was eye-opening. I felt like I was on an emotional roller coaster, but once I got off, I knew this is what my mama would have wanted me to do with my life. Last night reminded me of how much she used to love hearing me sing. I had forgotten that."

"It sounds like Michael knew what was best for you," Mary says, glancing over at the still quiet Jack. I blow him a playful kiss, and just like that, a forgiving air enters the space and we all take a moment to inhale it.

"Yes, he did. Although I have to admit that I wasn't too keen on the spotlight at first."

"It sounds like he *wants* the best for you, too. I, for one, think that's a good thing. Don't you, Jack?"

"He wears hard-bottom shoes, so you know he's all right in my book," Jack says, entering the conversation.

"Jack," I say cautiously, hesitant to bring up what could start another disagreement. "I've been thinking.—Most of the jazz restaurants will only need me Friday through Sunday. That means that I can still work here during the week."

"You're not changing my mind, Mýa."

"I have to agree with Jack," Mary says as she takes my hands in her own. "You will burn yourself out trying to do both."

Sensing that I'm still not going to win this one, I give in. "Okay. No working here once I find something. Just remember I still have to pay my rent until then, so stop trying to fire me."

"I'm not promising anything," Jack says with a dimpled smile.

Mary claps her hands together, glad that Jack and I are smiling again. "Hey, I meant to ask you if you started journaling. Jack said he gave you one," she says as I take a seat on the floor.

"Every night since Jack gave it to me. Don't worry; this whole conversation is going to get journaled tonight. You can both count on that."

We all enjoy a moment of laughter because that's what families do together.

Chapter Twenty-two

August 3, 1994

I take a seat on the bus around six, exhausted from working the breakfast and lunch shifts, but determined to make it to the Goodwill near Perimeter Mall before they close. Michael and I are finally going to see David and Michelle's baby this weekend, and I want to make a good impression.

A lady in scrubs smiles at me as I lean my head against the window. She looks even more exhausted than I am.

Pain recognizes pain.

I remember when Michael said that, and as I sit here with swollen feet that ache to kick my shoes off, all I can think about is finding the perfect dress to wear for him this weekend. Jack would have a field day with my thoughts right now. He'd probably say that I'm the one who will be saying "I love you" to Michael before we hit date number six.

An hour later, as the bus pulls up to the Goodwill shopping center, I can't help but wonder if he'd be right.

I rush over to the dress section the moment I hit the store, knowing that I have less than an hour to search through a hundred dresses and find what I'm looking for. A white lady with fiery red hair is digging through the dresses, too, and talking to herself.

"I can't believe some of these dresses still have the tags on them," she says, pulling out a blush sequined dress. She then throws it into her buggy, which already appears to hold at least ten other dresses.

"You must have a few special events coming up," I say. "All the dresses in your buggy look perfect for a formal affair."

She glances up at me. "No, these aren't for me. I'm looking for dresses to serve as costumes. This is the fourth Goodwill I've been to today."

"You're getting costumes for a play, or something else?" I ask curiously.

She pulls out a stunning red strapless dress, and we both take a moment to admire it before she tosses it in her buggy with the others. "I'm the costume designer for a new musical that's opening up at the Alliance Theater."

"That sounds like fun. That red one is beautiful."

"It is, isn't it? I'm getting dresses in different sizes since I don't know who our lead singer is going to be. I got a call this morning that the young lady we offered the part to turned it down, so now we're back to auditioning. I hate sitting through hours of auditions, but the director insists that everyone be a part of the entire production process."

"None of that sounds good," I say, continuing my own search.

"It happens. That's the nature of the beast in this business, but we'll find someone. We already have another casting call out."

"What kind of musical is it?"

"It's a jazz musical."

A shiver runs down my spine. *Jack will kill me if he finds out that I didn't say something.*

My hands begin to shake, so I rest them on top of a nearby clothing rack. "Where are the auditions being held?" I ask as casually as possible.

She stops her search. "Why? You sing?"

Say yes. Say something, girl. Don't just stand here like a deer caught in headlights.
"I—I do, but I've never done any acting."

"Neither had the girl we were trying to cast, but this part is strictly for a role as a jazz singer in a local club that the main characters go to throughout their courtship. It doesn't require acting, just a great voice. Who's your favorite jazz singer?"

"Nina Simone."

She gives me a quick once-over, as if she can tell whether or not I can sing just by looking at me. "You certainly have the look the director is going for."

I stand up straight—like it makes a difference.

"I need to hear you sing, of course."

Instantly, my knees go from a wobble to a wild and uncontrollable knocking.

Please don't let her hear them.

"I can sing something for you," I say faintly. "Do you want to go outside?"

"Why do we need to go outside? The audience isn't going to be outside; they will be staring right in your face. Thousands of them."

Please don't ask me to sing in front of all these people.

"Go ahead. Sing your favorite Nina Simone song."

Too late.

I take a deep breath and glance around the store, praying that the few shoppers I see browsing the nearby racks won't take notice once I start to sing. "Okay. I'll sing 'Blackbird.'"

"Perfect," she says as she reaches in her purse and pulls out a tape recorder.

This just went from bad to worse. "Wow, you keep a tape recorder in your purse?"

"I can't live without this thing. I use it to remind me which characters and scenes I'm shopping for," she says as she turns it on and then holds it up close to me. "Ready when you are."

I close my eyes and begin to sing the moment I hear her turn the device on. By the time I hit the second note, I no longer care that a recorder is hovering in front of my lips, capturing each lyric that I breathe out.

All I see in the darkness of my mind is Nina Simone, standing on a stage and dressed in all black with gold chains gently draped over the front of her blouse. I see her big afro and that soulful look of life upon her face as she sings about the loneliness of a mother and the pain of a father. I hear her rhythm as she digs deep into the tragedy of a blackbird that had no one to hold it and no one to love it.

I was that blackbird after Mama died.

I open my eyes and watch as my audience of one turns off the recorder just as I bring the song to a close. She says nothing, but the applause of those who stopped to listen gives me hope.

Feeling silly and unsure of myself as she places the recorder inside her purse, I wonder if I should ask something, say something, or just run out of the store. At this point, I'm leaning toward running.

What if she hated it?

"You have a voice. That was most impressive, and if I'm being honest, you sound better than the girl we had cast."

Don't scream. Be calm.

"I'm Francine, by the way," she says, offering me her hand.

"Mýa. Nice to meet you," I say, reaching for her hand and hoping that by the time the connection is made, mine will have stopped trembling.

We both stand there for a second or two, listening to a voice on the overhead speaker alerting shoppers that the store is closing in thirty minutes.

"I guess that's my cue to get going. It was nice meeting you, Mýa," she says as she reaches into her purse again and pulls out a piece of paper and a pen. "Come to this address on Friday. I'll arrange for the director to see you at six thirty in the evening, sharp."

I almost reach out and hug her when I take the piece of paper and slip it into my purse. "Thank you so much, Francine. I will be there."

She glances at her watch. "I need to get going, but I'm glad I happened to stop here when I did. I look forward to seeing you on Friday. Please don't be late."

"Me, too, and I won't be late. I promise," I say as I feel every bone in my body light up with joy.

I watch as she walks away with her buggy full of dresses and it dawns on me that I could be the one wearing that red dress if all goes well on Friday.

As I frantically search through the dresses, a fifteen-minute warning comes roaring out through the overhead speaker. I grab a tea-length black dress with gold buttons going down the front of it, squealing when I see that the dress's original price was more than two hundred dollars.

At the register, I hand the cashier a twenty-dollar bill with a big smile on my face.

Chapter Twenty-three

"Mýa, it's three o'clock. You need to get going. I don't want you to miss your audition. You know how bad Friday afternoon traffic can be," Jack anxiously shouts as he glances at the clock and then points to the front door.

I understand his concern. I have been watching the clock slowly tick the day away, and Michael has called more times than I can count to make sure I'm leaving at exactly three.

"We're going!" Mary shouts back as we rush toward the door.

"Mary, I can't thank you enough for driving me home. I don't think I can deal with the bus system today," I say, throwing my purse over my shoulder.

"You know Jack wouldn't let you get on that bus today if it were free," Mary says, opening the front door.

"Wait!" Jack shouts as he rushes over and gives me a bear hug. "I'm so proud of you."

"I haven't gotten the part yet, Jack."

"It doesn't matter. You're going for it, and to me, that's what counts. Nothing good in life happens without action. Besides, I already know you're going to get it."

"You do, huh?"

"I do. Remember, I've heard you sing," Jack says with a proud smile as he releases me.

"I'm so nervous."

"That's normal," Mary says with a wink. "I always say a little nervousness never hurt anyone."

Jack quickly glances up at the clock on the wall above the counter. "You're sure Michael will be at your place by five thirty to take you over there?"

"Stop worrying. Michael will be there, and the location is less than a twenty-minute drive away."

"Well, if he can't make it for some reason, Mary or I will come. We'll stay here until you call and tell us he's there. We can get over to your place in less than ten minutes if need be."

"He'll be there, and if he's not, I can hop on the bus. You and Mary go home, and I'll call you once my audition is over. Please, Jack."

"Nope. We'll stay right here until five, and that's the way it's going to be."

"You are so stubborn."

"I'm not stubborn, just firm." Mary and I both look at him until he relents. "Okay, maybe I am a little stubborn," Jack admits as everyone steps out from the kitchen to wish me well.

"Here goes nothing," I say, waving to everyone as Mary and I scurry out the door.

Chapter Twenty-four

Michael knocks on my door at five-fifteen.

"You're early," I say as I close the door behind him.

But he's not listening; he's staring at me with wide, dark eyes. "Wow."

"What?" I ask, rushing to grab my purse.

"That dress is stunning on you."

"I'm glad you like it because you'll see it again. I bought it to wear to meet David and Michelle tomorrow."

"You trying to get their baby to marry you? Because David is already hitched," he says with a coy smile.

I tug at my dress. "Is it too much?"

"No, I'm just kidding. It's perfect. I love it, and I can't wait to see it on you again tomorrow."

I notice an envelope in his hand. "What's that? Don't tell me it's another jar of Vaseline."

He hands the envelope to me. "Funny. It's something for you to give the director."

I open it and pull out a photo of me leaning up against Michael's car. "This is amazing," I breathe.

"You can write your details on the back and use it as a headshot."

I feel tears welling up as I look at it. "I've never seen myself like this."

"I told you that you are beautiful. Now you can see it for yourself."

"That sounds like the lesson you wanted me to learn at Marco's."

"If it worked, why not use it again? That's my motto."

I hug him. "Thank you. It's beautiful."

"Glad you are finally drinking your own Kool-Aid and liking the flavor."

"That's a good way to put it," I say. "It sounds like something Jack would say."

"My mother used to tell me that," he says, leaning over and kissing me.

"What was that for?"

"Nothing. I've been waiting to kiss you all day."

"Is that right?" I say, easing out of his arms so we can get going.

"You don't believe that I think about you when we're not together?"

I see the concerned look on his face as he waits for my response. "It's just weird to know someone other than Jack and Mary is thinking about me."

"I'm glad that I'm in such good company, but I hope that you think about me as well."

"I do. Too much, probably." I glance down at my watch. "We need to get going."

"I'm ready when you are."

"I just need to grab one thing," I say as I rush over to my kitchen table and grab the resume that Mary typed up for me earlier, sliding it into the folder along with my photograph. "I feel so professional. Although I'm afraid the director is going to look at this and just see that I have no experience."

"The part is for a jazz singer, not an actress. So the focus is on what you do best: sing. Who knows? You just might surprise yourself and turn out to be a great actress by the time it's over."

"I doubt it," I say, firmly closing the door behind us.

"Stop doubting yourself," Michael says as we make our way down the stairs.

"That's a hard habit to break," I say just as we reach his car.

"But one that you *need* to break," he says as he opens my car door. "Just remember that you can do anything that you put your mind to. I believe in you, but that means nothing if you don't believe in you, too."

"I'll get there."

I slide into the passenger's seat, but Michael's words linger well after he closes my door. It wasn't that long that ago that Jack said something similar.

You've got to do better. I pull the photograph out again and stare at it. *That's you, girl. Dark and—dare I say—beautiful.*

"This is the first time I've seen my mother in my eyes," I say.

Michael gives my hand a quick squeeze and then gets us on the road. As we come to a traffic light, he asks, "What song are you going to sing for your audition?"

I barely hear him as I continue to stare at the photograph.

"You still living over there?"

I jump like I've been pinched out of a dream. "I'm sorry."

"You nervous, or just thinking about something else?"

"Both."

"You want to talk about the 'something else' that's on your mind?"

"Not right now."

"I understand. In that case, I asked what song you think you're going to sing."

"'Blackbird.'"

"That's a good one. I think Nina Simone released it in 1963."

"I didn't realize you knew so much about her."

"I knew a little, but since she's your favorite, I went to the record store and the guy there told me about her whole career."

Could this man get any better?

"I wish I could come in and hear you sing it. I want to be there to support you."

Yes. Yes, he can.

"Maybe they will let you sit in the back."

"I wasn't sure how you would feel about it."

I reach over and place my hand on the back of his neck. "I want you there."

"You keep rubbing the back of my neck with those warm hands of yours, and I'll have to pull this car over and kiss you again."

I remove my hand, and we both laugh. "Then let me stop, because we can't be late."

Chapter Twenty-five

Ttttt

The director doesn't look anything like the person I had imagined when I met Francine.

Amelia Lang is tall, size two slim, and her hair is cut in a neat bob that touches the base of her neck. With honey-colored skin, high cheekbones, five-inch stilettos, tailored pants, and a matching cream silk blouse, she looks like she belongs on a runway rather than in a director's chair.

I'm glad I wore this black dress.

Michael and I take a seat in the back of the auditorium as I watch Amelia give an actor feedback on his audition. Her voice is kind, but it also doesn't leave room for you to miss her point. Everyone listens—not because she's the boss, but because she makes you feel like you are the boss, too.

I spot Francine in a pair of jeans and a pink blouse. Her fiery red hair is pulled up into a bun and she waves at me as Amelia begins offering feedback to another actor.

"This is intense," Michael says as Francine makes her way toward us.

"Mýa, so glad you made it. Are you ready?"

I stand up. "Is it okay if my boyfriend waits for me here?"

She looks at Michael and smiles. "I'm sorry, but we don't allow anyone inside except those auditioning."

"Understood," Michael says, quickly standing up. He kisses me on the forehead and then exits the auditorium.

"I'm sorry about that," Francine says as I fidget with my dress. "Did you bring a resume and headshot?"

"I did, but my resume doesn't show that I have any experience," I say, holding the envelope tightly in my hands.

Francine tugs on it until I get the hint and hand it over. "The director is looking for a voice that can bring this musical to life. I wouldn't have brought you here if I didn't think your voice could do that," she says, placing the envelope under her arm. "You're going to do fine. Just sing for her the same way you did for me."

"I can do that," I say as I follow her down to the front.

"I know. Like I said, that's why you're here. Amelia, this is Mýa, the young lady that I met at the Goodwill."

Amelia extends her hand to me. "I listened to your voice on Francine's little recorder. More importantly, I want to hear more."

"Thank you for the opportunity to audition," I say, trying not to squeeze the mess out of her hand as I shake it.

Amelia pulls her hand away gently and smiles. "Relax. I'm sure Francine told you that I'm looking for natural talent. You've already shown that you have that; that's why you're here. Now I just want to see you under the lights and get a feel for your presence on stage. Okay?"

"Okay. I'm sorry. I'll get it together, I promise."

"You'll feel better once you're up on the stage," Amelia says as Francine pulls my headshot and resume out of the envelope and lays them on a table next to us. I just stand there, smiling like an idiot.

"That's your cue to head on up, Mýa," Francine says patiently.

"Right. I'm sorry."

I make my way to the center of the stage as Amelia and Francine take their seats behind the table. A young man comes up and takes a seat at the piano that's off to the stage's side.

"What are you going to sing?" Amelia asks as she glances at my headshot.

"'Blackbird.'"

"Perfect. You can start when you're ready."

I inhale slowly and then turn to signal the pianist.

Just let go.

As I exhale, I open my lungs and allow the music to guide me. The lyrics of the song float through the air, bounce off the old walls, and then come back to me just when I need them. They pull at my heart, beg me to let go. And I listen.

The piano blends in with my voice and pushes me to sing with a passion that surprises me. The rich melody whispers something that only I can hear. It tells me not to be afraid.

And for the first time, I'm not. For the first time, I feel myself drinking my own Kool-Aid, as Michael put it, and loving the flavor. I open myself up to a life that seems to have chosen me.

As I bring the song to an end, I'm struck with the idea that, whether I land this part or not, tonight, here on this stage, I have done something great.

Chapter Twenty-six

I find Michael in his car with the seat back. He's fast asleep, so I tap on the window and watch him slowly open his eyes.

"So?" he asks as I put my seat belt on.

"They said they would call tomorrow if I got the part."

"How do you think you did? Wait, don't answer that. I already know," he says as he drives out of the parking lot.

"No, you don't," I joke.

"Yes, I do. I know you killed it, and I know that they will be calling you back because they would be crazy if they didn't. And for the record, that director didn't look crazy."

"She was beautiful," I say as I lean back in my seat.

"She was okay."

I give him a wry smile. "Whatever. You know that woman was beautiful."

"I was listening to how she spoke more than anything."

"Yeah, I was impressed by that, too."

"But, yes, she was beautiful," he says with a sly smirk on this face.

"What am I going to do with you?"

"Go to the park?"

"Now?"

"I know it's late, but I want to show you something."

"Okay, but we need to find a pay phone first so that I can call Jack and Mary. I know they won't go to bed until they hear from me."

"You can use my cell phone. I picked it up this morning. It's a Nokia, and it cost me a fortune, but I need it for my business. Frankly, I'm tired of using those pay phones to call a client back every time my beeper goes off."

"I didn't know that you have a beeper. Makes you sound fancy."

"I hate it, to be honest. I leave it at home because David made me promise that I wouldn't bring it on any date that I had with you because of the whole 'I work too much' thing. I'll be sure to give you the number to my phone and my beeper tonight."

"I think I'm really going to like this David. I can't wait to meet him."

"They're excited to meet you as well, and the baby has his ring ready."

"That's right. My future husband."

"You got jokes tonight. I like it."

"Where's the cell phone?" I ask, excited to try it out.

"In the glove compartment."

I open his glove compartment and pull out a black phone that when you flip it open, you can see all the numbers. "I don't even know how to use this thing."

"Just enter the phone number you want to connect to, and then hit the green 'talk' button. When you're finished speaking, hit the red 'end' button. Then flip it back down."

"Okay, here goes," I say as I carefully enter in Jack's number.

"It's not going to bite," he says as he glances over to find me gingerly holding it to my ear.

"Keep your eyes on the road, mister. I've got this. I think." I jump when I hear Jack's voice come through the speaker.

Michael bursts out laughing.

"You got it, didn't you?" Jack asks confidently, as if it wasn't even a question.

"I don't know yet, but they will call those who got parts tomorrow." Omit: "So, if they call, then I assume that means I got it."

I can hear Mary in the background, yelling that she knows I will get it.

"Why does it sound so windy?" Jack asks.

"I'm calling you from Michael's cell phone. He just got it today. We're headed to the park now."

"I see. Well, I know those things run by minutes, so we won't keep you. Have fun tonight, and don't come in tomorrow."

"Jack, tomorrow is Saturday—the busiest day for us. Not to mention that I had last Saturday off."

"So, now you'll have had two Saturdays off in a row. We'll survive tomorrow, so stop worrying. Just let us know the moment you hear anything."

"I will."

"Good night, kiddo."

"Good night, Jack." I hit the red button to end the call, flip the phone closed, and then place it back in the glove compartment. "Well, it looks like I have tomorrow off."

"Even better. I don't have a house showing until ten. We can hang out all night."

"Not *all* night."

"At least until the sun comes up," Michael says, another sly grin on his face.

Chapter Twenty-seven

Cars are everywhere when we pull up to Piedmont Park.

"Wow, I've never been down here, and I certainly never knew it got this busy on a Friday night. How are we going to find a parking spot?"

"A client of mine works here. I sometimes come early in the morning to take photographs. He lets me park in the employee lot."

"That's nice," I say as we turn into the employee parking lot and quickly find a good spot.

"It is, although I haven't been here in a few months. And before you ask, I haven't brought another woman here in years."

"I wasn't going to ask."

"But you were thinking about it."

"No, I wasn't," I say. He looks at me skeptically until I cave with a shrug. "Okay, so maybe I was thinking it a little."

"What am I going to do with you?"

"You could kiss me," I suggest.

"You don't have to ask me twice."

"I hear music," I excitedly say as we get out of the car.

"They have concerts all the time, and I know the perfect spot to sit and listen to them."

"Lead the way," I say, slipping my hand into his.

Ten minutes later, we come to a bench that's off the beaten path and surrounded by trees with branches so long that they look like they can reach out and hug you.

"You're right; this is a perfect spot."

"I'm glad you like it. The best part about it is that you are far enough away to have some space from everyone else, but you can still hear the music," he says as we take a seat.

I get a good whiff of the night air, allowing it to fill my lungs with happiness as the warmth of Michael's hand rests nicely upon my shoulder.

"What's your favorite color, Mýa?"

My eyebrow lifts as I look up at him. "Where did that come from?"

"From wanting to know everything there is to know about you."

I look into his eyes, and I see oceans of tomorrows in our future. "Blue. My favorite color is blue. What about you?"

"I'm more of a neutral color kind of man. Earth tones. But I think my favorite color is green."

"Why, because it's the color of money?"

"No, because that was the color of the water that I saw the first time I realized how much I loved photography. It was bluish-green, actually, but my camera picked up more of the green."

"That sounds beautiful."

"It was beautiful and a moment I will never forget."

"Jack always says that life is just seventy or eighty years made out of moments."

"I like that. Okay, I've got another question for you."

"I'm listening."

"What's your favorite flower?" he asks as the smooth harmony filling the air relaxes me.

"The orange lily. My mama brought them home one day. One of her patients gave them to her. I've been in love with them ever since."

"Nice. I've taken some photographs of that flower. I'll give you a few."

"I'd like that."

"Last question."

"I feel like I'm in an interview."

"Consider this good practice for when you become a big jazz singer."

"That'll be the day."

"It'll happen."

I bring his hand up to my lips and place a kiss on it. "Okay, what's your question?"

"How many kids do you want? Or do you want kids at all?" he asks as his fingers touch the side of my cheek, causing me to nestle myself even closer to him.

"I think I'd like to have kids one day. Two or three, but I also think I'd rather have a dog first."

"A dog?"

"Yes. When I was little, I used to beg my mama for a dog, but she said we couldn't afford it because dogs love spaghetti and meatballs, too."

"That's funny," he says with a chuckle.

"You laugh, but she really did say that."

"I believe you, but it's still funny."

"My mama had a good sense of humor," I say as the band begins to play a slower instrumental version of "Heaven Knows" by Luther Vandross.

Michael stands up and holds out his hand. "Dance with me?"

"Okay."

I stand, drape my arms around his neck, and allow myself to fall into his rhythm. His skin is so warm I can feel it on my chin as I place my head on his shoulder.

And he smells like...like a crisp summer night.

"We need to stop having starry nights like this, Michael. I'm beginning to think you're doing it intentionally."

He looks down at me. "Then you'd be right."

"Why? It seems like a lot of trouble."

"Getting my woman to fall in love with me is worth it in my book."

"So, that's your plan? For me to fall in love with you?"

"I want you to be where I am."

I stop moving altogether. "Are you saying that—"

"That I'm crazy about you? That you're sexy, beautiful, and highly talented? Yes, I'm saying that I'm falling in love with you."

I place my finger on his lips. "Then I'm where you want me to be, because I'm falling in love with you, too."

He pulls me so close I can feel his breath on my neck as we move with the music.

"I'm glad we got that out of the way," he says.

Chapter Twenty-eight

T he phone rings and I almost hit the floor.

"Good morning, Mýa. You okay?"

"Yes. Yes. Sorry, I was trying to grab the phone before it stopped ringing. Good morning, Francine," I say, recognizing her voice.

"Are you ready for some good news?"

I sit on the edge of my bed and rub my eyes. "Of course."

"The director loved you. Congratulations, you got the part!"

"Are you serious?"

"I wouldn't be calling you at eight in the morning if I wasn't. And since you were my discovery, I'm glad I get to be the one to do it."

"Right. I'm sorry, I'm just excited. Thank you so much, and please tell Ms. Lang I said thank you as well."

"I will. Come to the same place where we held auditions; we'll be there until at least nine or ten tonight. We'll get the paperwork done, discuss the pay, and get you a script. Rehearsals will start in two weeks. We run about three a week, and they'll be pretty intense. When you come for rehearsals, you will need to be off-book. That means that you will need to know any songs you're supposed to sing by heart. Will that be a problem? I know you have a full-time job."

"Not at all."

"Perfect. From here on out, the stage manager will be your point of contact. She'll be able to help you with anything that you might need." Francine takes a breath. "I know that sounded like a mouthful. I hope you got it all."

"I'm too excited not to. I feel like I'm hanging on your every word."

"I remember that feeling from when I got my first callback so many years ago. It's good to hear that things haven't changed that much since then. Congratulations again, Mýa. I'm looking forward to getting you in that red dress."

"Me, too."

I hang up the phone and practically hit the ceiling jumping for joy, causing my friend the spider to move a little in his web.

"I got the part!" I yell at him.

My hands shake with excitement as I dial Michael's home number.

He's probably just getting to sleep. The two of us literally stayed at the park until the sun came up.

I smile as I let the phone ring a few moments longer. My thoughts linger on the way he held me last night. The way he said, "I'm falling in love with you." The way my insides melted when he called me sexy. Truth be told, I was mad when the sun came up.

He must be knocked out. Hanging up, I grab my purse off the nightstand and pull out his pager number.

Ten minutes pass, and I start to worry, so I dial his cell phone and let it ring way longer than I should.

I'll try him again later.

I stare up at the spider on my ceiling and whisper, "You're the only one that knows." Then I pick up the phone and call Jack at the restaurant.

"Hey, kiddo. You got the part, didn't you?"

"I did. I have to go and sign the paperwork today. I'll see if Michael can swing me by there before we go to meet his friends."

"Mary and I said you'd be calling early this morning. But you don't sound too happy about this. What's wrong?"

"Actually, I'm thrilled, but I'm also worried. I've been trying to reach Michael to tell him, but he's not answering his phone."

"Maybe he's a hard sleeper."

"Maybe. I wouldn't know, but I wish he'd answer."

"Glad to hear that you don't know. That was a test."

"Jack, I need you to be serious."

"I am. Give Michael some time to sleep; he'll call. Maybe he had to go deal with a client this morning."

"I hope that's the case." I know Jack can hear the hesitation in my voice.

"What aren't you telling me?"

"Michael told me that he's falling in love with me."

"I knew it. What did you say?"

"I told him the truth."

"Which was?"

I bite my bottom lip while I weigh my words carefully. Admitting what I'm feeling inside for Michael isn't easy for me, and yet, I know I have to say it out loud. I can't allow fear to hold me back from love. "That I feel the same way," I finally say.

"Mary called that one. So, what's the problem, kid?"

"Maybe he realized that—hold on, someone is on my other line. It might be him."

"Okay, call me back after the breakfast rush—"

I switch to the incoming call before Jack is done talking. "Michael?"

"Yeah, it's me."

"I've been trying to reach you." I can hear something in his voice—something like tears. *Did he find out about my past?* "What's wrong?" I ask as calmly as I can.

"They lost the baby."

It's the last thing I expected to hear. I sink onto my bed.

"I'm so sorry, Michael. I want to be there with you. I'll catch a cab or call Mary, but I promise I will be there as soon as I can. Where are you? At their house?"

"I'm at the hospital." He pauses, and my heart sinks. "I didn't even get a chance to meet him, and now it's too late. He's gone. He's *gone*, Mýa."

"You being there for David right now means so much to them, I'm sure. Which hospital?"

"Emory. The one on Clifton."

"Okay, I'm calling Mary. I'll see you soon."

Thankfully, when I call the restaurant, Mary picks up.

"Mary, I need your help."

"Sure, honey, what do you need me to do?"

"Michael's friend, David, the one we were supposed to go see today—well, they lost the baby. Michael is with them at Emory, and I want to go and be with them, too."

"I'm so sorry to hear that. I'll grab my keys and come right over."

"Thank you."

Everything seems to be spinning out of control as I rush around, trying to throw on the first clean pair of jeans I can find. Well, clean enough, anyway. Fifteen minutes later, Mary pulls up, so I grab my purse and rush out to meet her.

"I feel so bad for Michael's friends. Losing a child is the hardest, most gut-wrenching pain to get over. It's like a wound that never quite heals. Even with time, you still feel its sting," Mary says with great sadness in her voice as we hit the expressway.

When I look at her, I see tears in the corners of her eyes. "Mary?"

I see her jaw clench as her hands tighten around the steering wheel. "I'm sure Jack never told you that we lost our child."

My eyes lower and my heart reaches out to her. "No, I didn't know that. I'm so sorry, Mary."

"It happened about six months after she was born. Jack and I had just celebrated our fifth anniversary. Her name was Violet because she had a birthmark on her foot that looked just like a flower. She was beautiful, and Jack—well, Jack was so proud. So proud to be a father. I never told him that I didn't want kids, but I swear all I could do was love her when I laid eyes on that child.

"She had light brown eyes and curly hair like Jack's: jet-black and beautiful. When she smiled, your heart melted. I knew the moment Jack had that little girl in his arms that she would be spoiled rotten—rotten to the core. He bought that girl everything. Things she didn't even need. Her room was filled with junk, everything from Atlanta Braves baseball caps to baby dolls. But I didn't care. She was our baby girl. I still can't believe Jack and I managed to create something so beautiful. I used to sing to her every night. I bet you didn't know that I can sing."

I shake my head.

"I can. Not like you, but I can hold a note, as Jack says. For a white man, he's always loved music with soul. He said it was the same way he liked his woman."

"I can hear Jack saying something like that," I say, happy to see a smile form on her face, even if it was only there for a second.

"When the doctors told us about her heart condition, we couldn't believe it. We almost spent our life's savings trying to find a doctor that could do something to save our child. Jack was even willing to sell the restaurant, but I wouldn't let him. When the reality hit us both that there was nothing we could do, I'd never seen Jack cry so hard. The death of our Violet almost ended our marriage."

I glance over at her in shock.

"It's true. We didn't speak to each other for days after we buried our Violet. We grieved so much apart that we forgot how important it was for us to grieve together. While I miss her to this very day, I'm glad Jack and I found our way back to each other before it was too late."

"I am, too," I say as she dabs her eyes.

"I'm glad you want to be there for Michael. When someone you love hurts, you hurt, too. Michael is going to need you."

"I can't imagine not being there for him. David and his wife are the only family Michael has. They mean so much to him."

"Well, now Michael has Jack and me, too."

I reach over and squeeze her hand.

"I was supposed to go and pick up the script and the paperwork later today. I'm not sure how they are going to feel about me not showing up."

"Call them when you get a moment and ask if I can go and pick up whatever it is that you were supposed to get. I'm sure once you explain the situation, they will understand. When does rehearsal start?"

"In two weeks. They will be held in the evenings."

"That's good. We'll have to talk Jack into letting you work the break-fast shift once the rehearsals start."

"Yeah, I'm sure I'm still going to need to work. I can't imagine the pay will be enough not to," I say as we pull into the hospital's parking lot and

Mary navigates to the front entrance to drop me off. "I'll call Francine from Michael's cell phone if he has it. I'll let you know what they say about you coming by to pick up everything."

"Okay. Hug Michael for us, and if that couple needs anything, you let them know that we would be happy to help."

"I will," I say, jumping out of the car and then quickly making my way inside.

—~~~~~·

My heart breaks the moment I catch sight of Michael sitting in the waiting room. His eyes are red, and he still has on the clothes he wore last night. He stands up as I approach him and wraps his arms around me.

"I won't ask how you're holding up," I say as we separate, and I take his hand in mine.

"I look that bad, huh?"

"You look like a concerned friend," I say, giving his hand a gentle squeeze.

"Thanks, I appreciate that."

"Do you feel like talking?" He slowly nods, so I ask, "What happened?"

"The unthinkable."

I wipe away the tear that falls down the side of his cheek.

"Michelle had just finished feeding the baby, and when she went to stand up and put him back in his crib, she started hemorrhaging so bad that her legs gave way and she dropped the baby. They say...they say that the baby died instantly. Michelle is still fighting for her own life."

I wrap him in my arms and hold him as tight as I can.

"What if David loses them both?"

"We'll be here for him, no matter what happens."

"I love you," he says as he rests his head on my shoulder. "Thank you for coming."

"I love you, too."

I watch people come in and out of the waiting room as Michael and I sit and wait. When I glance up at the clock, I see that it's almost three.

"Do you want some coffee?" I ask Michael as I stand up to stretch.

"I could use a cup."

"Okay, I'll go find us some and I'll see if they have anything for you to eat. I'm sure you haven't eaten anything since yesterday."

"Thank you. I'm starving."

As I head down the hallway, I spot a pay phone and call Francine.

"Don't tell me you've changed your mind," she says the moment she answers the phone and hears it's me on the other end of the line.

"No, it's nothing like that," I say, pausing for a second to clear my throat. "I'm not going to be able to come by this evening and was wondering if I could have a dear friend of mine come by instead. I'm at the hospital with my boyfriend."

"Is everything okay?"

"We're supporting a friend of his that just lost his son and his wife is not doing so well."

"I'm so sorry to hear that. I'll let the stage manager know that someone will be coming by on your behalf."

"Thank you. It will either be Mary or Jack who shows up; they are like my parents."

"Sounds good. The stage manager will be on the lookout for either one of them."

"Thanks, Francine. I really appreciate it."

"No problem."

After hanging up, I quickly call Jack, and then go look for coffee and food.

Walking back into the waiting room with a cup of coffee and a turkey sandwich that I got out of a vending machine, I see Michael speaking with a man that I assume is David. I search both of their faces, relaxing only when I see a slight smile on Michael's face as he hugs David.

Both men stand as I approach and ask, "How is she?"

"She's still in the ICU, but the doctors think the worst is over," Michael says with a glance at David, who nods his head in agreement.

I hand Michael his coffee and sandwich, but he turns and puts both down on a chair behind him.

"You must be Michael's Mýa." David says. "I hate that I finally get to meet you under these circumstances."

"I'm so sorry for your loss. If there is anything I can do, please let me know."

"Thank you." David says with a tremble in his bottom lip. Michael places his hand on his shoulder, providing a small measure of comfort. "Thanks, man. Right now, I'm just trying to get my wife to rest. She won't stop crying, so they're going to give her something. But she's like me, so I know she won't take it. She keeps saying it's her fault, but it wasn't. The doctor called it PPH. He said it could happen to any woman, and up to twelve weeks after giving birth. I still can't comprehend it all, but it took the life of our child and almost took my wife from me."

"Is it all right if I go see her?" Michael asks as he stands up.

David slowly nods as his tears hit the bare white floor.

I want to reach out and hug David, but I'm not sure if that would be appropriate. Instead, I tell Michael, "I'll stay with David."

"Thank you. I'll be back."

David and I watch Michael go through the waiting room doors.

"Do you want to sit and maybe eat Michael's sandwich?" I ask.

"I'll sit, but I'm not very hungry."

"I understand," I say as I pick up Michael's coffee and sandwich and take a seat.

David leans back in his chair and rests his head up against the wall. As he closes his eyes, I notice that he has a more mature look than Michael. There are a few wrinkles around his mouth and eyes, so I assume he's older than Michael. His hair is neatly trimmed. I glance down at his shoes and notice how polished they are. His tailored black dress pants have a serious crease in them, and you can tell that at one point, his white collared dress shirt was perfectly starched. It barely moves. Michael also looks and dresses nicely, but David seems to take it to another level. The expensive gold watch on his left arm confirms that.

"Is that Michael's coffee?" he asks as he slowly sits back up.

"It is. He hasn't drunk out of it, if you want it," I say, handing it to him.

"Thank you." He takes a few sips. "I can't believe this is happening. Last night, we were holding the baby and joking around about which of us he looks like. Today, he's gone. *Gone.* How do you deal with something like that?"

"One minute at a time."

"Justin Montgomery Myers. Do you know how long it took us to come up with that name?" He smiles faintly. "Michelle and I debated almost every day. It was fun because it was all done in love. Love for him. I had just bought him his first little football helmet. Now, he's never going to get a chance to wear it. My mind still can't accept—"

"David, come quick! It's Michelle!" Michael shouts as he bursts through the waiting room doors.

David jumps to his feet, and within seconds, he and Michael disappear from view.

At one o'clock in the morning, as I sit in the waiting room and watch others sink into uncomfortable hospital chairs with tired eyes and worried hearts, Michelle's blood pressure drops to dangerous levels.

At 1:15 p.m, her body goes into shock.

By 1:45 p.m., on a day that should have been filled with sunshine, David has lost both his son and his wife.

Chapter Twenty-nine

Michael and I sit on the sofa at David and Michelle's house, exhausted. It's taken us hours to get David to a place where he can think straight, but he finally listens to us and goes to his room to get some sleep.

"I can get a cab home," I say after closing my eyes for a few minutes. "I know you don't want to leave David alone."

Michael takes my hand in his. "Why don't you sleep here? You can stay in the guest room and I'll sleep on the couch." He looks into my eyes and I know he can see the hesitation written there. "Don't worry. I'm old-fashioned, but you can still lock the bedroom door if that would make you feel better."

I give him a wry smile as I allow his suggestion to roll around in my head for a second. "Are you sure David would be okay with that?" I finally say, still not quite comfortable with agreeing to stay in the home of a man I just met, someone who just lost everything that he lived and breathed for. But while Michael keeps staring into my eyes, I feel the anxiety that I'm having about all of this relax some.

"I am sure," he says. "Besides, it's too late for you to take a cab back downtown."

I glance down at my watch and reluctantly agree. "I'll stay."

Jack is going to have a fit when he finds out.

His smile reaches his eyes. "Thank you," Michael says, leaning back against the sofa. "Now I don't have to worry about you being in a cab at midnight."

"I can't believe it's that late," I say as my body finally begins to settle down.

"Yeah, it's been a long day," he says as he looks at David's closed door.

"I'm glad he finally agreed to take the sleeping pill the doctor gave him. Tomorrow is going to be even harder for him."

I shake my head. "I don't think he took the pill. I think the weight of everything just finally got to him. But you're right. Tomorrow will be even harder."

Michael's shoulders drop and his body sinks deeper into the sofa. "I know I said this earlier, but having you here means so much to me."

"I wouldn't have wanted to be anywhere else," I say, even though I'm still worried about the fact that Jack will have words with me about it tomorrow. But I know I'm where I need to be.

"I can't believe we have to plan two funerals," he says with a long sigh.

"I can't believe it, either. I'll help in any way that I can, and I know that Jack and Mary will want to help as well."

"Thank you."

"I'll fix breakfast in the morning. I hope he'll eat something," I say as I remove my shoes.

"He probably won't. You know how it is."

"I do." I say as I tuck my legs underneath me.

"I've never had your cooking," Michael says.

"I hate that it's under these circumstances."

"Me, too."

"Mary will want to prepare a few meals. Are you going to stay here for a couple of days?"

He nods slowly. "I think I should. I'll clear my schedule for the next week. My clients will understand."

"You don't have any closings?"

"No, thankfully." Michael allows his eyes to close as silence falls over us. His jaw clenches and I take in the grief upon his face as he sits, clearly deep in thought. I reach over and take his hand in my own. "They say that losing a child is the worst kind of pain. David's heart is not just broken from losing his son; it's shattered into so many pieces from also losing his wife. I can't walk in David's shoes, but I understand the size and the weight of them. I think I told you that I had to bury my brother right after burying my mother."

"I remember, and that's why I'm so glad that he has a friend like you in his life."

"We're like brothers, you know. I need to be strong for him, help him get through this, but I don't know if I can."

I reach over and hug him. "We'll both help him."

He places his hand on the back of my neck and then lightly kisses me. His tears fall on my own cheek. "You got the part, didn't you?"

"I did," I say as I wipe his tears away.

"That's my girl."

Stretching out on the sofa, he places his head on my lap and closes his eyes again. I feel the pain inside of him like it's my own as he tries to rest.

When someone you love hurts, you hurt, too. Mary's words linger in my mind as I close my eyes.

Chapter Thirty

T he sun warms my skin as I slowly open my eyes. I look over and see David sound asleep in a chair across from us, his legs and feet propped up on the coffee table.

He didn't want to be alone.

I ease my way off the sofa, gently lay Michael's head on a cushion, and then head off to find the kitchen, desperate for a cup of coffee.

The kitchen, with its white walls, high-end stainless steel appliances, and beautiful black floor tile, is the cleanest and most organized kitchen I have ever seen. Even the black and white kitchen towels are neatly folded next to the faucet. I quietly open a few of the white cabinets and find everything I need to start a coffee pot and fix a couple of omelets, bacon, toast, and a small pot of oatmeal. While I wait for the water to boil, I use the phone on the kitchen wall to call Jack and Mary and let them know where I am. I'm not surprised when Mary tells me that she's already started to prepare a few meals for David, but I am surprised when Jack doesn't say anything about me not going home last night.

Fifteen minutes later, I have the oatmeal, toast, and a couple of omelets done. The bacon is just about ready for me to pull out of the oven when David walks into the kitchen. He sits down at the table and rubs at his bloodshot eyes.

"You want a cup of coffee?" I ask, feeling weird about being in their kitchen, cooking in their pots and pans, all while knowing that the woman who usually does this sort of thing for him is gone.

"Please," David says.

I pour him a cup and wait for him to ask why I'm in his wife's kitchen, touching all the things that she probably touched just a day or so ago.

"You know, Michelle didn't know how to cook. In fact, she never came in here unless it was to sit at this table and wait for me to bring her breakfast—whenever we had a chance to eat together, that is." He looks over at me. "Poor thing couldn't even boil water."

I can't help but laugh, and it's good to hear him join in.

Michael walks in, rubbing his eyes as well. "David's right. I remember that time when I tried to show Michelle how to cook for their anniversary. She threw her hands up after only a few minutes and said, 'I'll order something and David will love it even more.'"

"I remember that. Michelle tried to act like she had slaved in the kitchen all day. She even had on an apron when I got home to make it look authentic."

"She loved you so much, man," Michael says, sitting down at the table across from David.

"Yes, she did. I'm going to miss her so much, Michael."

"But you will never forget her. Those memories will always be in your heart, and they will help you get through this. So will I."

"Thank you, man."

Michael looks up at me and smiles as I place full plates down in front of him and David.

"I can't believe I'm starving," Michael says, but I know he's just saying it to encourage David to try and eat something.

We both watch David pick up a piece of toast and take a few bites. Both of us smile when he eats a small portion of his omelet and a spoonful of oatmeal.

After we finish eating, I clear the dishes, wash them, and carefully put them back where I found them while Michael and David sit at the table drinking coffee and sharing stories about Michelle. It's interesting to see this side of Michael. As I watch him comfort his friend with so much sincerity and patience, it makes me realize something. *I could marry this man.*

—⧸⧸⧸⧸⧸—

"I'm going to go take a shower," David says an hour later. "I also need to call Michelle's parents and her sister." He can barely haul himself out of his chair and my heart breaks again as I watch Michael help him up.

After David leaves the room, Michael walks over to me and wraps me up in his arms. He holds me tightly. "Thank you for the breakfast."

"You're welcome."

"I can run you home now, if you want."

"Mary prepared a few meals for David, so I hope it's okay that I told them that they can bring them over before heading to the Braves game. They're also going to bring me Mary's car."

"That's very nice of them."

"They want to help any way they can."

"I wish you could stay here tonight as well."

I give him a kiss. "I need to get home, shower, and get ready to head back to work. Unfortunately, no matter what a person is going through, the bills don't stop or care."

"That's so true," he says, disappointed.

"I will call you later this evening. Okay?"

"Okay, but I think I need a longer kiss if I'm not going to see you for a couple of days."

"If that will help."

"It so will."

Chapter Thirty-one

Monday morning brings mixed emotions with it. I walk into Jack's with the strangest desire to call Francine and tell her that I can't do the musical. I haven't even opened the envelope that contains the script. Michael and I spent last night on the phone, so now my eyes are straining to stay open as I sit at the table and stare at a plate of food I have no desire to eat. To make matters worse, one of the cooks casually mentions that we're going to be shorthanded today for lunch, so I know that in less than five minutes, Jack will ask me to do both shifts.

As if on cue, he walks into the back and takes a seat.

Right on time.

"I can tell you're tired, kid, but I need you today."

"I heard."

He reaches over, pats my hand, and then heads into the refrigerator to pull out the bacon.

As I pour my coffee, I can't help but think about Michael and David. I know my not getting any sleep doesn't come close to what they're going through by making the funeral arrangements today. So I force a smile on my face as I put on my apron and name tag.

Jack taps me on the shoulder as I sit at the table, resting my eyes for a second or two before the lunch rush begins.

"You look exhausted, kid, but thanks for doing a double. I know you would rather be at home."

"I'll be okay. I will probably sleep like a log tonight."

He grins. "No, you won't. You'll be up all night on the phone with Michael."

"You're probably right," I say with a sigh.

"Come out back for a second. Mary and I have something that we want to show you."

I can barely get my body to move as I follow him out the back door, looking around for something different or new, but all I see is Mary standing by her little blue Honda.

Jack hands me the keys. "It's your car now."

I stare at them in disbelief. "Are you serious?"

"We are. You'll have to pay the insurance, of course, but I figured with the gig you got, you can use that money to pay the first six months up front. By then, you should have something else coming in. I'm sure the insurance payments won't be much since it's old and paid for."

Mary walks over to him and crosses her arms. "Are you referring to the car or me?"

Jack winks at me. "I've learned never to answer questions like that and expect to live—or eat, for that matter."

"What's Mary going to drive?"

"I don't need to drive. Besides, Jack and I are always together, so we really only need one car. We should have done this before now."

I hug them both. "You guys are amazing. I love you both so much. Please know that."

"We do know—that you love us and how amazing we are," Mary says as she starts to walk back inside the restaurant.

"Now you can get home, even when it's late," Jack says with a pointed grin.

"I slept on the couch."

"I know. Michael made a point to mention it when we dropped off the meals for David." He places his hand on my shoulder. "I know you're grown, that you're twenty-seven, but I can't help that I'm just old-fashioned that way."

"So is Michael."

"I knew there was a reason why I liked that young man."

There's a ton of reasons why I like—no, love—that man.

I hug him again. "Thank you for the car, Jack."

"Anything for you, kid. Absolutely anything."

Chapter Thirty-two

The week flies by quickly as Michael continues to help David get things ready for the funeral.

I sit at my kitchen table listening to Nina Simone while eating a grilled cheese sandwich that I brought home from the restaurant. My open window allows a gentle Friday night breeze to come in. I find myself missing Michael something fierce. We talk on the phone every night, but it isn't the same as feeling his arms around me or just being near him.

It's funny, really—or sad, if you dwell on it—but for four years, I've spent my Friday nights alone and thought nothing of it. However, now everything is different.

I'm different.

I'm—dare I say it out loud?—in love.

Four weeks ago, you couldn't have convinced me that I, Mýa Denise Day, would be cruising down Love Lane and hoping that there aren't any detour signs or potholes along the way.

Jack says I have it bad, and I can't disagree with him. The only thing that seemed to be getting me through the week is going over my lines. They keep my mind busy, for the most part.

However, I'll admit that two nights ago, I almost purchased one of those bridal magazines.

It was a very close call.

I never thought memorizing songs would be so hard, as I go over each of the songs that I'm to perform in the musical. When my phone rings, I'm grateful for a break from going over each of the songs that I'm to perform in the musical. I hope that it's Michael calling to give me the final funeral details.

"Mýa, it's Francine. Sorry to call so late."

"It's fine. Everything okay?" I ask, placing my script on the table.

"No, it's not. The stage manager was going to call you, but I wanted to tell you myself."

My knees start to tremble. "Tell me what?"

"The show has been canceled."

"Why?" I ask, trying to keep my emotions in check as I press the phone closer to my ear.

"Money. The producer didn't get the expected funding."

"How could they let things get this far if they didn't have the funding secured?"

"In this business, everything is done on promises and dreams. Some come true, and some fall through. That's the way it is. I'm so sorry. If I hear of anything else, I'll let you know."

"Thank you for calling me and letting me know."

"Before I hang up, I want to tell you that I'm going to mail you that red dress."

"You don't have to do that, Francine."

"I know, but that dress is too beautiful to end up back at the Goodwill. I'll get it in the mail tomorrow. You should have it in a couple of days. Take care of yourself, Mýa. You have a beautiful voice, so don't let this stop you from doing something with it."

"I won't," I say, hanging up the phone and feeling the weight of disappointment deep down in my gut.

How am I going to tell Jack?

"Hey kid, what's going on? Did the funeral time change?" Jack asks.

"No, everything is still the same: two o'clock tomorrow. I'm sorry to call at this time of the night; I know you and Mary are usually already in bed."

I hear the sounds of sheets rustling and a switch being flipped.

"What is it? You sound like you've been crying."

"The musical was canceled," I say while trying to choke back tears. "I got the call about twenty minutes ago."

"I'm so sorry to hear that, but don't let this deter you from pursuing your singing. There are always going to be mountains along our path, Mýa. You just need to figure out how to either get over or around them."

"When Francine first told me I got the part, my initial reaction was that maybe this was too much," I say, wiping a tear away and sitting up straight in my chair. "But now I want this. I want to sing. Not because I believe the world deserves to hear my voice, but because *I* deserve to hear my voice."

"It's good to hear you say that. You can do it, kid. Just remember success is not about making it big with others; it's about making it big with yourself."

"You always know what to say, Jack. I don't think I could do this without you."

"Mýa, you have your own strength. True, Mary and I can be a support system, but the foundation of what keeps you pushing through tough times has to come from you. I may not always be around, you know. That's how life goes."

"I hate it when you talk like that."

"Reality, kid. Just reality. Hold on. Mary wants to talk to you."

I wait as he passes her the phone.

"I'm so sorry about the show being canceled, Mýa. You'll find something else. Something even better."

"I hope so," I say, switching the phone to my other ear.

"Hope is how dreams become a reality, isn't it? Hold on, here's Jack again."

"Hey, kid. Try and get some sleep, and we'll see you tomorrow. We'll pick you up about fifteen minutes after twelve."

"Michael is glad that you guys are coming to the funeral."

"I know. He called to thank us just after dinner today."

"He did?"

"He did. He's a good guy."

"Yes, he is."

"Glad to hear you say that, and out loud this time. Now, get some sleep, or at least let me get some. This old man needs his beauty rest. I'll see you in the morning."

"Thanks, Jack."

"You're welcome, kid."

Chapter Thirty-three

T he funeral home is packed. As I look around and admire all the flowers that grace the room, I can't help but feel good seeing that so many people loved Michelle and have come to show David their support.

I wish I had met her and the baby.

Michael is still having a hard time forgiving himself for not seeing Justin right after David and Michelle brought him home. I know only too well that no one can convince someone else to forgive himself or herself for something like that. Forgiving yourself is one of those things that takes time. Sometimes, it never happens. As Jack would say, that was reality.

I spot Michael talking to a beautiful woman who's as tall as he is, and I try to fight off the sting of jealousy that creeps into my bones as I help Mary and Jack find seats toward the back. I relax some when Michael spots me and waves me over.

"Jenna, I would like to introduce you to my girlfriend, Mýa." She extends her hand and I feel my foolish bout of jealousy fizzling out as we shake politely. "Jenna is Michelle's older sister."

"Half-sister, but like Michelle always said, family is family," Jenna says to me.

"I agree. To Michelle, you were simply her sister from another mother," Michael says.

We enjoy a brief moment of laughter, but I see the sorrow of losing a loved one hovering around the corners of Jenna's eyes.

"It was a pleasure to meet you, Mýa. Now, let me go find David and see if he's ready to get started."

When she's out of earshot, Michael leans over and whispers in my ear, "I see you're wearing that black dress I love."

"I told you that you would see it again."

"I needed something to make me smile today, and seeing you in that dress is doing it," he says, moving closer to me. "I've missed you something fierce. I hope that doesn't scare you."

"Not at all. I felt the same way all week."

"You just gave me a reason to smile today."

I catch something in his eyes—agony, of course, is there, but there is something else, something I can't put my finger on.

"I'm so sorry I didn't call you last night, Mýa."

"It's okay. I understood, and I didn't call you because I wanted to let you get ready for today. I knew how hard it would be."

"Last night was probably the roughest, but I still want you to know I was thinking about you. Focusing my thoughts on you was the only way I could finally get my mind to rest."

I reach out and wrap his hand in mine. "Did you get any sleep?"

"Not much. David didn't get to sleep until around four this morning. Then he was up at eight, staring at Michelle's pictures and holding a teddy bear that he had bought for the baby. I can't tell you how long that image will be in my head."

"A tough sight to see, no doubt. So, you're going to stay at David's place a while longer?"

"For another week, at least. I want to be there for him after the funeral. That's when everyone else goes back to a normal routine, but for the person going through a storm like this, nothing is normal for a long time."

It takes all I have not to kiss him as my tears fall. "I'm so glad he has you."

"And I am glad to have you," he says, wiping away my tears and making me love him even more. "No one should go through something like this alone. I know what that feels like, and I won't allow it to happen to him."

"Jack and Mary are here as well," I say. He takes a quick look around. "They're sitting in the back. It's crowded in here, so you probably can't see them, but we'll come up after the funeral is over."

"You're going to sit with me, aren't you?"

"Do you think that's okay? I mean, I'm not family."

There was that look again.

"I know David wouldn't have it any other way. Neither would I, for that matter. I need you by my side."

I reach up and touch his cheek. He grabs my hand and places a light kiss on my palm. "Okay, I'll sit with you. Let me go tell Jack and Mary."

"Thank you. I think I'll go and take a seat myself. We should be starting soon."

"Sounds good. I'll be right back."

Just as I get back to where Jack and Mary are sitting, I see him.

He looks older, of course, but I'm sure it's him: the younger police detective who questioned me that night, the one with the black mole on his cheek and the thick eyebrows. My knees are barely able to hold me upright. My heart begins pounding so loudly that I'm quite sure everyone around me can hear it.

"What's wrong, Mýa?" Mary asks as Jack follows my gaze across the room.

"You see someone over there that you know?" Jack asks as he reaches out, grabs my trembling hands, and pulls me down into the seat next to him. "Who?"

"One of the detectives that questioned me when I was arrested. He's the one with the black mole on his cheek and the gray suit," I say, reaching down to physically stop my knees from trembling.

Jack finds who I'm talking about and looks him over. "Are you sure?"

I nod.

"What's he doing here?"

"I don't know. He's sitting in the back, so I can only assume that he's not family, but he must know either David or Michelle."

"Do you think he recognized you?" Jack asks while glancing at the officer again.

"He probably didn't see her. And even if he did, think of how many people he's probably questioned since that night," Mary says in a low tone.

"Mary is right."

"I hope so," I say, trying to get myself together. "Anyway, I can't worry about it now. Michael wants me to sit with him. Is that okay with you guys?"

"Sure, honey," Mary quickly says. "It's probably better that way, anyway."

Jack nods in agreement and tries to give me a comforting smile, but I know he's just as nervous about the situation as I am.

"It'll be okay, Jack. If he recognizes me, he recognizes me. I'm here for Michael."

"I agree. We'll see you after the service is over."

I make it to the front of the room and take my seat next to Michael just as David steps up to the podium. I try not to peek back to see if I can find the detective in the crowd, but I can't help it. My nerves have gotten the better of me and now he's all I can think about.

Michael glances at me and whispers, "You okay?"

I nod my head and force myself to focus on David as he speaks about the woman and child he loved more than any of us could imagine.

———≋≋———

"Let me go and grab Jack and Mary so they can say hello before they head out."

"Okay. It was a beautiful service, wasn't it?" Michael asks with teary eyes.

I hug him. "It was."

"Jack and Mary can come to the repast if they want."

"I'll let them know, but I'm sure they want to let just the family be with David."

"They are family."

I slide my arms around him as we stand there, locked in a moment of grief. Wishing there was more I could do to comfort him, I reluctantly let him go and say, "Let me go see what they want to do."

A friend of David's that Michael also knows walks over and I use this moment to slip away and cautiously head toward Jack and Mary. Scanning the crowd as I go, I look for the detective. I spot him by the back door, holding a woman's hand.

The only way you're going to know if he recognizes you is to just walk up to him and see if he tries to put you in handcuffs.

I know I'm being silly. I also know that he can't arrest me, but I'm afraid he'll do something worse, like tell someone here how he knows me.

With just a few steps between me and the detective, I glance over and see Jack and Mary watching me. The expressions on each of their faces tells me that I should abandon this foolish plan of mine, but it's too late. The detective and I make eye contact when I find myself standing in front of him.

"Hi," I say. "You look familiar. Have we met?" His girlfriend, I assume, looks me up and down as I hold out my hand.

"I get that a lot," he says as he takes my hand and gives it a polite shake.

"Did you know Michelle?"

"I did," his girlfriend chimes in. "Michelle and I went to school together when we both lived in Chicago. How do you know her?"

I turn and point to Michael. "That man right there is David's best friend. He's also my boyfriend."

Her smile grows wider and more genuine. "I see. He's handsome. I bet you two look good together."

"I hope so."

"Well," she says, "my husband and I need to get going. We've got a flight back to Chicago to catch. We moved back there a couple of years ago."

"One day, maybe Michael and I will get to visit Chicago. I hear it's beautiful. I hope you two have a safe flight back."

"Thanks." They turn and make their way out the door as I take a moment to calm my nerves and catch my breath.

"That was bold of you," Jack says from just off my left shoulder.

"I figured it was the only way to know for sure."

"Did he recognize you?" Mary asks, anxiously.

"He didn't seem to, which is good, but my poor nerves are still a mess."

"I'm sure," Jack says, staring at me. "I know what you're thinking."

"You're going to tell Michael about your past, aren't you?" Mary asks, not missing a beat.

"Today made me realize that I need to. There are five years of my life that he doesn't know anything about."

"I don't think you should, but we can talk about it later," Jack says.

I nod. "Michael wants you and Mary to come to the repast."

"Isn't that for family only?" Mary asks.

"Michael said you are family."

"We would love to go, but I'm tired," Jack says as Mary reaches for his hand. "It's been a long day."

"I understand. I am, too, but I have to go. Michael would be furious if I told him that I wasn't coming."

"We'll tell him that we can't make it," Jack says as we begin making our way to where Michael, David, and Jenna are standing.

Jack is going to try to talk me out of telling Michael, but I can't let him. Right?

Chapter Thirty-four

"My decision is final," I say as I plop down on the sofa at Jack and Mary's house, waiting for Michael to arrive for Sunday dinner.

"You don't have to do this," Jack says, taking a seat in his chair.

"I do. Look, Jack, since you and Mary were wonderful enough to give me the car, the least I can do is pay for the insurance up front, like we discussed."

Mary sits on the sofa with me. "But why do you want to take money out of your savings when you can just pay it on a monthly basis like Jack suggested? You've been saving that money since you started working for us so you could buy yourself a house."

"Mary is right, kid. You wouldn't even take some of it out to buy a sofa to sit on, and now you want to pull out such a big amount."

"I've decided to buy one of those as well." They look at each other with concerned expressions, and I rush to reassure them before they can get carried away. "Don't worry. I'm not going crazy. Yesterday just made me realize that while it's great to save for the future, it's also good to enjoy some of the present. I'm not saying that I should have a 'just do whatever I want' kind of mentality, but I do want to enjoy a few small tokens of my hard work now." I can tell by their incredulous expressions that they're getting ready to dig into me some more, and I'm thankful that the doorbell rings just in the nick of time. "I'll go answer that."

"We're not done with this conversation," Jack says as I jump up to answer the door.

"Hi," Michael says, looking handsome in dark jeans and a sport coat. "I hope you don't mind that I brought David."

I hug David. "Of course not. Jack and Mary will be thrilled."

"Hey, why does he get a hug before me?" Michael complains as he and David step inside.

"Because when I hug you, it might take longer. And I'm hungry," I say with a sly smile as I close the door.

"It smells delicious in here," David says, pretending he didn't hear my comment to Michael.

Mary's face lights up when she sees him. "Welcome to our home, David. I love your black suit; it fits like it was tailored just for you."

"Actually, it was. Thank you, and thanks for allowing me to crash your family dinner," David says, shaking Jack's hand. "And thank you again for all the prepared dishes."

"Family is always welcome at our home," Jack says as he gestures for everyone to head to the dining room table.

I give Michael a quick hug before we trail after the others.

"Finally," he says. "I hope a kiss will follow that later."

"After dinner, maybe."

"Well then, let's get that out of the way."

"Michael, maybe you can help us settle something," Jack says, just as we get ready to dig into dessert.

I give Jack a look that clearly says I don't want him to bring this up now, but he ignores me.

"Sure. I'd be happy to help."

"Mýa's been saving up to buy a house, and now she wants to use some of that money to pay six months of insurance on the car that Mary and I gave her. Now, I realize that we're not talking big money here—a thousand dollars or less—but Mary and I feel that she needs all of her savings for a good down payment on the house she wants. You're a real estate guy; what's your take on this?"

"I thought you were using the money from the musical to pay for the insurance?" Michael asks me as I glare at Jack for bringing up the insurance again, not to mention I hadn't told Michael about the musical yet.

"The musical was canceled," Jack says bluntly. "That's why we want her to pay for the insurance monthly. That way, she doesn't have to touch her savings."

"Jack," I say as calmly and respectfully as I can. "I'm not a child, and I don't need you to try and dictate every step that I take. It's my money, and I will do what I want with it. I may decide to not even get a house, but that's my decision to make. If I wanted Michael's opinion, I would have asked him for it. And for the record, I hadn't told him that the musical had been canceled, but thank you for doing it for me." I get up from the table and storm out the front door for some air.

"Hey, wait up," Michael says as I make my way down the stairs. I stop and wait until he catches up to me, then we begin to walk together. "Why didn't you tell me the musical was canceled?"

"I got the call Friday night. I didn't want you to worry about that. You already had enough on your plate."

Michael pulls me into his arms. "I'm so sorry, Mýa. I know that must have hurt when you got that call."

"I cried for twenty minutes, but I know I will find something else. I'm determined to do so."

He pulls me closer to him, and his hand moves up the small of my back as he holds me. "I hate that you went through something like that and I wasn't there for you."

"Michael, it's okay. I'm okay. You know Jack gave me a good pep talk."

"I still wish I could have been the one to do that. I love you."

When I look into his eyes, I see the truth of those words. "I'm ready to give you that kiss now."

"Good, because I didn't get dessert."

I laugh, but as he leans over to kiss me, a raindrop hits me on the shoulder. "Did you feel that?" I ask, placing my hands on his chest.

"The only thing I want to feel is your lips on mine."

Another raindrop hits me on my forehead. And then another one. "Michael."

"Yeah, I feel them, too. We better get back. You're not off the hook, you know."

"I hope not," I say as I grab his hand and we run toward the house.

A light sprinkle begins to dot the sidewalk as we rush up the steps. Michael reaches out and grabs my hand just as I'm about to open the door. I turn around to see a nervous look on his face.

"Before we go back inside, I want to ask you something."

Is this it? I can already feel my lips parting, ready to scream "yes."

"Okay," I say instead, feeling a twinkle of excitement in my toes and not caring that the rain has begun to pick up some.

Michael clears his throat.

This is it. Brace yourself, girl. You're about to be on Marriage Lane.

"I—I wanted to ask you if you would like to go to the park with me next Sunday to take some photos."

What?

"I know it's a Sunday, and I know that you like to spend all day over here, but it would be early in the morning, around seven. That's the perfect time to capture the sun coming up. We'll finish with enough time to get over here by lunchtime, I promise."

I stand there, trying to find my tongue so I can give him an answer that will make any sense. "That sounds great. Looking forward to seeing you in your creative element," I finally say, hoping that I sound convincing rather than disappointed.

Looks like we're still on Love Lane. For now, anyway.

Chapter Thirty-five

"I'm sorry, Mýa." Jack says, the moment Michael and I walk back into the dining room.

I rush over and hug him. "I'm sorry, too."

"As Michelle would have said, family ain't family unless you're fighting," David says while he grabs a piece of Mary's homemade sweet potato pie and we all laugh.

"On that note," Mary says with a look of relief. "Let's put on some music and play some cards since there's no Braves game on tonight."

"You're a Braves fan, huh?" David asks Jack.

"Die-hard. Who do you like?"

"Michelle was from Chicago, so out of loyalty to my wife, I'd have to say the Cubs. But, I have always secretly been a fan of the Braves."

"I've always wanted to see Wrigley Field," Jack says.

Mary grabs Jack's hand. "Enough baseball talk. David, you keep this up, and you'll have Jack talking nothing but baseball all night. I want to play some cards, then I want to dance with this man of mine."

Jack gives Mary a quick kiss on the cheek just as I catch Michael and David whispering something to each other out of the corner of my eye.

What's that about?

"Michael, you want to help me take these dishes into the kitchen?" I ask. He nods and starts gathering the plates.

"I'll go and find us some cards," Jack says. "David, you like play spades?"

"No offense, Mr. Tanner, but you can't handle me at your spades table."

"Is that right?" Jack says with a smirk. "Mary, I think we're going to have to show David here how it's done."

"I believe we are," Mary says with a grin of her own.

"I'll be there in a second," I say, grabbing some plates off the table before following Michael into the kitchen. As soon as we're alone, I ask, "Okay, what's going on?"

"What do you mean?" Michael says, placing his dishes in the sink.

"Why did I get the feeling that you were going to ask me something else on the steps?"

"Because I was."

I knew it!

I try to keep my hand from shaking as I adjust my grip on the plates in my hands. "So, what was the real question?"

He takes the dishes out of my hands and places them in the sink, too. "Can I have my kiss first?"

"Michael," I say anxiously.

"Okay." He moves closer to me and looks deep into my eyes.

Can he see me flying down Marriage Lane?

"My broker is having a formal dinner next Saturday, and I was going to ask if you wanted to go, but I know how last-minute that sounds."

"Oh."

"I'm sorry. I know I should have asked earlier, but considering the situation, I wasn't sure if I would even go. To be quite honest, I had forgotten about it."

"I would love to go." *I would love for you to ask me to marry you, but a formal dinner will have to do for now.*

"You could wear that black dress that you had on yesterday."

"You don't wear a dress like that to a formal dinner."

"Why not? I love that dress on you."

"I have something to wear, and you'll love it, too."

"I can't wait," he says. He leans over to kiss me just as Mary walks into the kitchen.

I can't help but laugh at the disappointment on his face. He gives me a kiss on the cheek and then dashes out of the kitchen.

"Me and my timing," Mary says as she walks over to the sink and puts the last few dishes in with the rest. "You okay, Mýa? You look more disappointed than Michael did just now."

"Yeah, I'm okay. It's just that I got the feeling that Michael was going to—"

"Propose?"

"I know how crazy that sounds, considering."

"Considering what?" she says, filling the sink with water and adding a little dish detergent so the dishes could begin soaking.

"Considering it's only been a couple of weeks since we started dating."

"Mýa, I've learned a lot of things in my life. One of them is that you can't put real love on a timetable. It doesn't work that way. Love doesn't say, 'Since it's only been a few weeks, let me wait.' No, love happens at the very moment that it needs to happen."

"So, you don't think it's foolish that I thought he was going to propose tonight?"

"Why would I? You know, I never like to admit that Jack is right about anything, but he called it when he said Michael was in love with you the moment he heard you sing. He was in deep before then, but hearing you that night did something to that man, and he hasn't been the same since. You put it on him."

"Mary! I can't believe you just said that."

"What? How do you think I got Jack? Men need to see there's something unique about you. Something special. That's what draws them in."

"I can't believe we're having this conversation."

"Why? We're both grown, and besides, you felt the same way that night. That's why you sang that song the way you did."

"I do love him, Mary. I love him so much that it scares me."

"Love is supposed to scare you. If it doesn't, you aren't doing it right. Now, come on. Let's go play some cards."

Chapter Thirty-six

I feel a wave of uneasiness come upon me as I walk into the restaurant. Everything seemed to be okay when I left last night, but still, I feel I need to be on guard and resolved to do exactly as I told Jack that I would regarding withdrawing money from my savings to pay for the insurance up front, and to buy myself a sofa.

"Hey, kid," he says as he looks up and takes a moment to stop cracking what seems to be over a hundred eggs.

"Morning, Jack," I say, searching his face for any sign that he's upset with me.

"Stop it. We're good. I was out of line last night and you had every right to remind me that I can't dictate everything step that you take in life. It's just hard, because to me—"

"I'm your daughter," I say, finishing his sentence for him. "I feel the same way, Jack. I love you and Mary; you're like parents to me. I don't want you to feel like I don't value your opinion or that you can't offer me advice."

"I know you love us, kid, and thanks for saying that you still want this old man's advice." He looks down at the bowl. "I think I've cracked enough eggs for today."

"I'd say."

We both look down at the bowl and smile, and I know that all is right in our world again.

"I meant to tell you that when Mary and I were on our way to the Braves game, we saw a billboard advertising a new jazz restaurant that just opened. It's by the Goodwill where you met Francine."

"The one in Perimeter Mall?" I ask, taking a seat at the small wooden table that Mary purchased a few years back so their employees would have somewhere to sit and eat in the kitchen.

"Yeah. I didn't mention it before because you already had a gig, but maybe you should check it out and see if they're looking for a singer. The billboard said that they're going to have a live jazz band."

"Do you remember the name of it?"

"Mary might." He yells for her, and she comes running through the double doors with a frantic look on her face. "Hey, Mary, do you remember the name of that jazz restaurant that we saw the advertisement for? You know that one I'm talking about? The one we saw on our way to the Braves game?"

"That's all you wanted?" she asks, slightly annoyed as she places her hands on her hips. "The way you screamed my name, I thought—never mind."

"So, do you remember?"

"I think it was called Jazzmyne's."

"Yeah, that's it." He looks over at me. "I knew she would remember. She's got the memory of an elephant."

"Are you calling me an elephant?"

"No! I...uh..."

She walks out of the kitchen and back up front before he can finish.

"I wasn't calling her an elephant," he says sheepishly.

"I'm staying out of that."

"Good call," he says. "So, what do you think? You going to check out that new place?"

"I'll give them a ring and see if they need someone. Thanks, Jack."

I watch as he puts foil over the eggs, hesitating with each of his movements. Something else must be on his mind, and a speech is probably brewing in that head of his.

"I was thinking about you buying a house. Maybe you won't have to go it alone."

"Jack." I know he's thinking that maybe Michael and I will get married and buy the house together, but I'm not ready for that conversation this morning. I haven't even poured myself a cup of coffee yet.

"All I'm saying is that maybe Michael wants to buy a house, too."

"I'm not saying it's impossible, but we haven't talked about that sort of thing yet."

"Let me ask you something."

"Sure, Jack."

"If Michael asked *the question*, would you say yes?"

"With all my heart, but I think that I need to tell him about my past before any of that is a possibility."

He looks around and spots a few potential eavesdroppers. "Let's go to my office."

I look at the coffee pot, realizing that I'm not going to get a cup anytime soon, but I follow Jack to his office anyway. I take my usual seat as Jack closes the door.

"I've been thinking about that, too," he says, moving some papers off his chair and then taking a seat. "After that situation at the funeral, when you saw that detective and all, I think maybe you're right. Maybe you should tell Michael about your past."

"I'm not going to lie, Jack, telling him scares the mess out of me. I'm not sure how he'll take it."

"What's there to take? Like I've said a million times, you were eighteen—young and dumb. I'm sure he'll see it that way."

"But people lost their lives that night, Jack."

"That wasn't your fault. That was all Zee. Look, kid, you didn't bring that gun, and you didn't pull the trigger, nor did you even know Zee had it. And let's not forget that you weren't inside when it all happened, or that you got out of the car to try to stop him. From my perspective, that blood is all on Zee, including his own."

"The judge disagreed. He felt that I should have gotten out of that car and gone to the police or someone who could have helped."

Jack slaps a hand on this desk. "I don't want to have *that* conversation again." When he sees me start to protest, he continues. "No, I'm serious, Mýa. Over the past four years, I feel like we've had that conversation more times than I can count. Even if you had gotten out of that car and gone

for help, it would have been too late, and you know it. Zee was going to
do what Zee wanted to do. You focus only on the past, and you never
look at what you've done since then." He points to the degree hanging
on his wall. "You went to school and got a degree. You work your butt
off six days a week, ride that stinky bus every day, and live in that crappy
apartment, all so you can save up enough to buy your own home, which
shows that you know you can have a better future. You have an amazing
voice, and you're ready to do something with it. And you're finally starting
to see yourself as a beautiful black woman. Like I've told you over and
over again, stop selling yourself short."

"You're right."

Jack stares at me, amazed that I agree with him. I'm amazed at myself.
But I feel like the light has finally been turned on in my mind and I get
what Jack has been telling me all along.

"I only hope Michael sees it that way, as well."

"Michael loves you. I'm not going to sugarcoat it and pretend like he's
going to be happy about it at first, but I trust that he'll come to understand it all as I do. It's your past, not his, and it all happened way before
you met him."

"What if I lose him, Jack? What if he can't get past it?"

"I'm going to tell you something, kid, something that I haven't spoken
about in years."

"I know about your little girl. Mary confided in me."

Jack looks down at his desk for a second. "Yeah, that was hard. But
what I'm about to tell you is not about that. It's about me."

I sit up in my chair to pay close attention.

"When Caroline broke my heart, I started drinking. One night, I left a
buddy's house, drunk as a skunk. I should never have gotten behind the
wheel, but there I was, at one o'clock in the morning, driving down this
little dark road. I didn't see that the car just up the way had stalled, and
by the time I did, it was too late. I lost control and slammed into a pole.
Thankfully, I got out of that car with the breath of life still in me. I spent
six months in jail and another six months doing community service. After

that, I couldn't get a job because I had a DUI on my record. My father didn't know what to do with me, so he brought me here, to my grandfather's restaurant. My grandfather gave me a second chance to do something with my life. When I met Mary, I told her all of that, and she loved me anyway. She didn't just look beyond my white skin; she looked beyond my past. She focused on the future she and I could make together."

I sit back in my chair again and think about Jack's story. "I hope it turns out that way for me."

"If Michael is a real man, it will."

"I love you, Jack."

"I know, kid. You still going to get your insurance today?"

"I am. And Michael and I are going to look for a sofa tomorrow."

He gives me a sour face.

"We're not fighting today, Jack."

He throws his hands up in the air. "Fine." Then, he opens his drawer, pulls out an envelope, and hands it to me.

"Jack, I can pay for insurance."

"It not for insurance or your sofa. I want you to get yourself a chair if you see one you like. That way, Michael has somewhere to sit when he comes by." He gives me a wink as I shake my head.

"Jack, you are a mess."

"So says my wife. Thankfully, she married me anyway."

Chapter Thirty-seven

The sun is still out even through it's eight in the evening. I walk into an old but well-kept building on Piedmont Avenue. The gold plaque on the door proudly states that the building belongs to David Montgomery, insurance broker.

His receptionist has already left for the day, but I find David in his office, staring at a picture of Michelle. I knock on the open door softly, and when he looks up at me, I can tell that he's been crying.

"You caught me," he says as I take a seat across from him.

"Maybe you need to give yourself more time before coming back to work."

"No. I need to get out of that house. Everything there reminds me of Michelle and Justin. Coming here allows me to focus on something else, like helping you find a great insurance company."

"Helping others always makes one feel better," I say, hoping it will bring even a faint smile to his face.

"Exactly. I know I'm still going to have moments like the one you caught me having just now. It's part of the healing process, as everyone keeps telling me."

I nod, wishing I could say something more, something comforting like Michael would. "So, what great insurance company did you find for me?" I say, hoping to at least lighten up our conversation some.

Finally, I see a smile. "One that you're going to love because they were able to give me a yearly rate for what you were expecting to pay for six months. Plus, they've been around for a long time and have the reputation to show for it."

"Sounds perfect."

David loosens his silk silver tie, leans back in his leather chair, and folds his hands on top of his antique desk. "You know, I've known Michael for a long time. Our broken homes were right next to each other."

"Michael told me that. I can relate to a *broke* home; my mama was a nurse and a single mother."

"I bet you remember making those mayo sandwiches."

We both laugh as I nod and say, "I do."

I ease back in my chair and wait for him to ask the question that's obviously lingering on the tip of his tongue.

"You know, Michael *really* cares for you."

I place my hands in my lap and look David in the eye. "I really care about him, too. I love him."

His shoulders relax. "I can tell, but as his best friend, I'm glad to hear you say it."

"You think Michael and I are moving too fast, don't you?"

"I'm a romantic. I wined, dined, and married Michelle three months after meeting her."

This time, I'm the one to relax. "Sounds like a great story that you're going to have to tell me some day."

He smiles. "I will." Then, he grabs a yellow file out of a basket on his desk. "Okay, let's talk more about this great yearly rate that I got you."

As I lean over to examine the documents, I can't help but smile at David. I can't blame him for taking our conversation where he did. It's what people who care about you do. I've learned that from Jack and Mary.

Chapter Thirty-eight

I hear Michael knocking on my door, so I grab my purse so we can head right out.

"No Nina Simone today?" he asks as I step out into the hallway and close my door.

"Not tonight. I'm too excited about going shopping," I say as a huge smile spreads across my face.

"I see that. I feel like we're going to get ice cream instead of a sofa."

"Come on," I say, gently pulling him toward the steps. "I want to have enough time to look around."

"Okay, I'm good with that. Cute dress, by the way. That pink color looks good on you."

"Thanks. I still haven't had a chance to do laundry, so I don't have any clean jeans." I glance over and notice that he's still in work attire. "Since you have on dress pants and a dress shirt, I guess I'm glad I didn't have jeans to wear."

"Yeah, I didn't get home in time to change. It's been a very busy day."

"I saw David yesterday. But he probably told you that," I say as we walk to his car.

"He did. I was surprised he went back to work so soon."

"I thought you were going back to your place after you left Jack and Mary's on Sunday."

"I was, but I think I need to stay a bit longer."

"Are you sure that's what he needs?" I ask.

"You don't sound like you think my staying is a good idea. I thought you understood why I'm still there."

I offer a neutral smile. "I can't say whether it's a good or a bad idea. I'm sure it's going to take David some time to get used to being in the house by himself."

"Last night he mentioned selling it," Michael says as we both put on our seat belts.

"You don't think David should give it some time? He might have different feelings about it in six months."

"Ultimately, it's his decision to make," he says with a slight frown.

"But you feel he should sell it?"

"It would sell quick. It's a great house that's been well cared for, and it's in a good Midtown neighborhood. I looked at the comps this morning; he would make a good profit from it."

"That was a little eager, don't you think?"

"Looking at the comps? I wanted to see what David's options are, just in case. Like I said, it's *his* decision to make."

I detect a hint of anger in his tone as he merges into traffic. "You sound upset with me."

"It sounds like you're suggesting that I'm putting ideas in his head just for a sell."

"I'm just asking questions. But, since you mentioned it, are you?"

"Of course not. I know David. He's not like me."

"What does that mean?"

"It can take me a minute sometimes to make a decision and act. David, on the other hand, just dives in, so I wanted to be ready and have something to show him when he pulls the trigger."

Is he trying to tell me he isn't ready to propose?

Michael exits the expressway and turns into the parking lot of the furniture store. We sit there for a minute or two, not saying a word.

"Did we just have our first argument?" I ask as I reach over and place my hand on top of his.

He grins. "I think we did."

"Good. I'm glad we got that out of the way."

"Look at you, using my words." He leans over and kisses me on the cheek. "You're so cute when you get mad. I hope you stay that cute after..."

"After what?" I ask when he doesn't finish his thought.

"After we've been dating a while."

I give him the side-eye as we get out of the car.

Chapter Thirty-nine

Picking out my new sofa doesn't take as long as I thought it would. A few minutes after entering the store, I spot the one I want. Thankfully, it's a floor sample and on clearance.

"You make buying a sofa exciting and quick," Michael says as we walk back to his car.

"I can't believe the great deal I got on it. I almost got the accent chair."

"Why didn't you?"

"You're right. I should have gotten it. Jack gave me the money for it so you would have a place to *sit*."

Catching onto my meaning, he chuckles and then grabs my hand. "Let's go back and get it then. For Jack, at least."

We both belt out a good laugh and head back into the store, much to the salesperson's delight. Twenty minutes later, we walk outside again with the receipts for the chair and the sofa stuffed into my purse.

"I can't wait for them to be delivered on Friday."

"It's ironic; they actually match the one chair that I have."

"Is that why you liked both of them so much?" I ask playfully.

"Maybe."

"We'll have to get them all together one day."

"We will."

This flirting with Marriage Lane is driving me crazy.

"Since you mentioned ice cream earlier, why don't we go and grab some?" I suggest.

We stand in front of his car, enjoying the evening air.

"I think I'd prefer some actual food. I didn't get a chance to grab lunch earlier, and my stomach is starting to remind me of that."

"That sounds even better. Jack mentioned this new jazz restaurant yesterday. It's in this area." I glance down at my watch. "It's seven thirty, so they should be open. Let's go and check it out."

"Maybe they're looking for a singer."

"That would be nice, but no dragging me up on stage this time," I say with a wink.

"Too bad I didn't know about this place beforehand. You know I would have called to see if I could arrange it."

"You are so much like Jack."

"I'll take that as a compliment," he says, unlocking my car door.

"It is. He's always looking out for me."

He nods his head in agreement. "We can use my cell to call information and get the address."

"Okay, where is it?"

"In the glove compartment."

"Great. I'll get it."

"Hey, wait," he says, stopping my hand with his before it can open up the compartment.

I look up at him curiously. "What's wrong?"

"I just remembered that I left it at David's. I'm still getting used to carrying that thing around."

"Okay, maybe we can see if someone inside knows where it is?"

"I'm sure they do. Let's go see."

A few minutes later, we have with the restaurant's address and are happy to learn that it's just around the corner.

Chapter Forty

S tepping into Jazzmyne's is like stepping into another world, one filled with cobblestone streets, soft candlelight, and crystal stemware. The atmosphere is a pleasant mix of classic jazz icons blended with a dash of country, blues, and funk influences. The vibe that seems to travel from table to table enters into my bones and makes them come alive. My eyes study the female waitresses dressed in all black with a silver brooch, and I admire the men who have on white bow ties to match their crisp white uniforms. Lights and crystal chandeliers line the ceiling, and pictures of musical legends hang on the walls papered in linen cream. As we head to our table, my ears tune in to the band that's on stage, belting out a fresh take on a Billie Holiday song.

"Wow. This place makes Marco's look C-rated," Michael says as we take our seats.

I gaze around the large space and nod. "It's definitely more upscale."

"The band even sounds better," Michael says, snapping his fingers to their harmonious beat. "That guy on the bass is bringing the funk."

"I didn't realize you were a guitar man," I say.

"I prefer the saxophone, but after tonight, I might be changing that."

"The food sounds appealing," I say, scanning the menu.

"I could see you singing here."

"That would be amazing, but I'm sure they have a long list of people trying to get this gig."

"That doesn't matter. The important thing is that they're not you." He reaches over the table and takes my hand in his. "I mean that."

"Thank you. I'm going to have to see about getting an audience with the owner."

"I'm sure she's here somewhere."

"I doubt she would want me engaging her in a conversation about a job during business hours."

"You never know. That's probably her coming up on the stage now," he says, directing my eyes to the front of the room.

"Good evening, and welcome to Jazzmyne's. I'm your host, Jazzmyne Mitchell. I thank each of you for choosing to visit our family tonight. Everyone you see on this stage has been with me for many years. We've performed locally and overseas, and I hope that you are enjoying what you're hearing. Here at Jazzmyne's, we play music that touches heart, mind, and soul."

My eyes follow her as she moves gracefully around the stage in a blush evening gown, commanding our attention. Her jet-black hair is tucked behind her ears in a sleek shoulder-length bob. Her deep-set blue eyes scan the audience as she rests her hands on the microphone. Her high cheekbones, skin that looks as if it has been gently touched by the sun, and slender nose calls the singer Vanessa Williams to mind.

"Did you know that each of you here tonight makes music? It's true. The beautiful sound you make when you put your hands together lets us know that you're feeling the lyrics that we're sending to your hearts. Can I get a little of that love now?" The audience responds accordingly. "Thank you. Now, I'm a firm believer in word-of-mouth advertising. That's how many of you heard about us. So, I'm going to share some information with you tonight. We're looking for a lead singer here at Jazzmyne's. Don't get me wrong. I love performing for you all—I do—but I need to ensure this place stays at the level you have come to love and expect, so it's time for me to pass this mic to someone else. If you know of anyone, send them to us and we'll see if their lungs can blow."

Michael stands up, but I slide down into my chair as the spotlight moves to our table.

"Looks like one of you out there is eager to share or sing. Which one is it, sir?" Jazzmyne asks.

"I don't sing, but this little lady crouched down in her seat can really blow."

"Is that right? Well, ladies and gentlemen, maybe we should turn this evening into an audition. What do you think?" The crowd began to clap again, so Jazzmyne motions for me to come up on stage.

Michael nudges me out of my chair. "Come on, show her what you can do. We may not get another opportunity like this."

I nod and head toward the stage.

When I join her, Jazzmyne looks me up and down. "You're a beautiful little thing, but can you blow?"

"I can."

"Nice. I like that confidence. What's your name?"

"It's Mýa."

"Well, Mýa, let's see what you can share with us."

Jazzmyne moves off the stage as I step in front of the mic and take a deep breath. "I'd like to sing something originally performed by Nina Simone. It's called 'Four Women.'"

<hr />

"That was nice," Jazzmyne says later as she shakes my hand. I search her facial expression as we chat, trying to determine if "nice" is good enough to get the gig or not. By the time she moves back to the stage, her unenthusiastic demeanor hasn't changed, and it's discouraging, to say the least. But she does call over her shoulder, "Leave your number before you leave."

"What did she say?" Michael asks eagerly as I return to my seat.

"Not much. Jazzmyne said my performance was...nice."

"She loved you."

"How could you tell?"

"I watched her as you sang. Her head was bobbing. You don't bounce like that if the music isn't moving you."

"I hope so."

"Look, if she doesn't call, we'll find something else. This is Atlanta. Music is happening here."

I take a sip of my water. "You're right."

"I wish I had a tape recorder to capture you saying that."

"You sound like Jack."

"I'm sure Jack yearns to hear Mary say he's right about something. Every man in love secretly wants to hear that from his woman."

"All I know is that it's been a loving battle between them for over forty years."

"One day I hope to be married as long as they have."

Just drink your water, girl, and smile. Smile a lot.

Chapter Forty-one

—̵⦇⦈⦇⦈⦇⦈—

August 20, 1994

There's a slight spring of excitement in my step as I walk into work, thankful that it's finally Saturday and that ten hours from now, I'll be slipping on that red dress to "put it on" Michael, as Mary had once so elegantly said.

As usual, I head to the kitchen to grab coffee and breakfast.

Speaking of Mary, she slides into the seat across from me as I sip on my coffee, trying not to stare at the clock, and eagerly asks, "You ready for tonight, Mýa?"

"Funny. I was just thinking about tonight."

"I'm sure."

We exchange a knowing glance, and I feel myself blushing.

"Come back to the office; I want to give you something." Mary stands and I follow her to Jack's office. She removes a box from the bottom desk drawer and hands it to me. "These will go perfectly with that red dress you told me about."

I slowly open it and gasp at the sight of a pair of dangling diamond earrings. "Mary, I can't wear these."

"Why not?"

"Are they real?"

"Child, there isn't a point in wearing anything else in my book. Not when you're going to an event like the one you and Michael are headed to tonight."

"They are beautiful."

"Jack gave me those when this restaurant started turning a profit. It was his way of telling me that he was glad that we made it happen together."

"I didn't know the restaurant was ever not making money."

"When Jack's grandfather passed away, his books and finances were a mess. But I was smart with the numbers, so Jack turned the financial part over to me, and he took care of getting the building and the menu up to par. Once people tasted Jack's food, they started coming back. We made a great team."

"You still do." I notice a hint of sadness behind her eyes. "Everything is okay with you and Jack, right?"

"We're as in love today as we were over forty years ago. Now, try on those earrings. I want to see how they look on you." Obediently, I take off my thrift store finds and put on Mary's earrings. She stands back to get the full view. "They belong on you, Mýa. Your short hair really helps them pop."

"I'll be sure to bring them back. I promise."

"I'm not worried about the earrings. I just want you to enjoy all that tonight will bring."

"I hope there's dancing. I'm wearing heels, but they aren't that high, just in case."

"Smart."

Jack walks into the office just as we get in a quick hug. "Oh goodness, I had to walk in when you two are having one of your moments."

"What moments?" I tease him.

"You know, those moments when women do all that hugging and crying stuff together."

"We do hugging and crying stuff together," Mary reminds him.

"We're married, and I'm forced to—it's part of the job."

"You are a mess," Mary says.

"It's taken you forty-something years to figure that out?"

"Of course not, but I married you anyway."

I watch them kiss, and it warms my heart. It reminds me of that picture that Michael took—the one he calls *Love Endures*. I don't know of another couple that fits that statement as accurately as Jack and Mary.

I pray that in forty years, Michael and I have that kind of love, that kind of spark.

He has to ask you first. Right.

Chapter Forty-two

Michael calls at seven o'clock, just as I walk into my bedroom.
"You ready?"

"I am. What time will you get here?"

"I'm downstairs."

"Why didn't you come up?"

"I wanted to see you walk down the stairs."

I hold the phone away from me for a second and take a deep breath before pressing the phone back to my ear.

"Are you blushing?"

"Just a little," I admit. "I'll be down in a minute."

"I can't wait."

"Stop it."

"What? What am I doing?"

"Making me nervous."

I place the phone back on the hook and slip into a pair of red satin heels. They set me back sixty bucks, but considering how comfortable *and* cute they are, I'm happy that I purchased them. I glance in the mirror, admiring how well my dress fits me; it's like it was tailored for my every curve. I love that it's not too tight or too loose.

Can I get a BAM!

I laugh at my own antics as I give Mary's earrings some love and then dab on my favorite gold eye shadow. Grabbing my purse, I make my way to the door, but stop and head back to my bathroom.

I open my medicine cabinet and pull it out—the small jar of Vaseline that Michael gave me. I apply a small amount over my neutral tone lipstick and then, take one final look at myself in the mirror. All of a sudden, it hits me; I wish my mama could see me tonight. Not just because

I'm all dressed up, but because when I look in the mirror, I see a woman with beautiful skin.

—❦❦❦❦—

"Close your mouth," I tease Michael as I slowly walk toward him. He's standing by his car, gaping at me.

"I can't. I think it's stuck, and I can't blame it. You look absolutely beautiful."

"Thank you. You look handsome in your suit. Are those for me?" I ask, pointing at the bouquet of orange lilies clutched in his hand.

"Yes. Sorry. I'm still trying to regain my composure," he says, handing me the flowers.

"These are beautiful, and they smell good," I say as he opens my door. Michael closes it behind me and then gets in the car, only to resume staring at me. "What's wrong?"

"Nothing."

I turn to my window and smile. *Mary would be so proud of me.*

"By the way," he says as we turn onto the main street. "I suggested to David that he give it six months before he makes a final decision about selling the house."

"What did he say to that?"

"He agreed."

"I know you only want what's best for him."

"I do, but you were right. He shouldn't make any major decisions right now. I moved back into my apartment last night, too."

"How do you feel about that?"

"I realized that David's not me. When I lost my mother and my brother, I needed him and Michelle close by. I crashed at their place for weeks. David is much stronger than I am."

"I wouldn't say that. You have your strengths, and the two of you have different ways of dealing with situations. It doesn't mean that one is stronger than the other."

"You're right."

"What was that?" I joke.

"I said, you're right, *dear.*"

"I could get used to hearing that."

His laughter makes my heart dream about forty years of laughter.

Chapter Forty-three

Whe stop in front of a three-story apartment building that looks very modern: crisp white paint on the outside, trimmed trees, and a lit hallway.

"Is this your place?"

"It is," he says as he removes his seat belt. "I forgot something that I'm supposed to bring for my broker. It will just take a sec. Why don't you come in?"

"You know, I've never seen your apartment."

"Well then, I'm glad we can get that out of the way."

"Funny."

"Come on up."

I follow him up the stairs, but he stops when we get to his door and looks back at me.

"Did you forget your keys or something?" I ask when I catch a glint of nervousness in his eyes.

"No, I have them right here. I just wanted to get another quick look at you in that dress."

"You are a mess," I say as he opens the door.

Michael wasn't kidding when he said he had no furniture. He did, however, have the chair that he mentioned, and he was right; it did match my sofa and accent chair perfectly.

"This is nice, big. But you were right. Your place is as bare as my own."

"I guess I was waiting."

"Waiting for what?"

"For the right designer." The sparkle in his eyes makes me want to kiss him. I step toward him and he grabs my hand. "I want to show you something. It's out on the balcony."

"Okay," I say, a little disappointed that I didn't get my kiss.

Michael opens the door to his balcony, and I'm surprised to see a saxophonist seated in the corner. He begins to play "Feeling Good" as I take in the orange lilies covering the floor, the soft lights draped across the balcony railing, and the candles spread all around us.

My eyes fill with tears. "It's beautiful."

"Dance with me," he whispers as he draws me close. I feel the gentle warmth of his fingers gracing the small of my back. "I hope you're not too disappointed that we aren't going to dinner."

I slowly shake my head as he kisses away my tears.

"I love you, Mýa."

"I love you, too, Michael—with all my heart."

The saxophonist stops, and Michael gently pulls away. "I want to ask you something."

"Okay," I say softly.

He reaches in his coat pocket and pulls out a black velvet box. I gasp for air as tears begin to stream down my face once again.

"From the first moment that I saw you walk into Marco's, I knew that I couldn't let that night slip by without approaching you. Since then, every day has been something I want more of. You were there by my side when tragedy struck. You're beautiful, and I love you so much. David will tell you that I'm not one to move quickly, but you make me want to do just that. I want to have you forever in my arms. I want you to marry me. I want to spend every day listening to that beautiful voice of yours. I guess what I'm trying to ask you is—will you be my wife?"

"Yes," I whisper as he opens up the box, takes my left hand, and places the one-carat engagement ring on my finger. "It's beautiful."

"A beautiful ring for the most beautiful woman in the world."

The saxophonist begins to play again as we slow dance to the soft melody.

"I can't wait to tell Jack and Mary."

"They know."

I pull back slightly, staring into his eyes with open curiosity.

"I had to ask Jack for your hand."

"When?"

"Well, I was going to propose at the family dinner on Sunday, but after you and Jack had a spat, I had to come up with something else."

"I knew it. You were going to ask me when we were standing on the steps, weren't you?"

"I was."

"And the ring, it was in the glove compartment that night when we went to the furniture store, but you tried to pretend you'd left your cell phone at David's house. Wasn't it?"

He nods and lets out a soft laugh. "But I think this way is much better, don't you?"

"You could have asked me covered in mud, but yes, this way is so much better," I say.

"Well, I'm glad we got that out of the way."

"Me, too."

"So when are you thinking would be a good time for the wedding?"

"Yesterday would have been perfect," I say as I rest my head on his shoulder and listen to the saxophonist transition smoothly into a lovely rendition of "When a Man Loves a Woman" by Michael Bolton.

Chapter Forty-four

"Michael, where's your restroom?" I ask when the saxophonist stops playing to take a break. "I need to go touch up my makeup after all this crying you have me doing tonight." I reach up and dab the corners of my eyes, which are now marred by tears and smeared eyeliner.

He brushes my cheek with the tip of his finger. "At least they're happy tears."

"Yes, they are the happiest of the happy tears," I say, glancing down at my ring again. "It is so beautiful."

"I'm glad you like it and I'm glad it fit. We have Mary to thank for that."

"Mary knows diamonds," I say. "These are her earrings."

"Then Jack knows diamonds, too."

I laugh. "I guess that's right."

"I can't wait to buy you a pair."

"I don't need diamonds. I already have you," I say.

"You're not going to get to the restroom if you keep talking like that."

"You're right. Which way is it?"

"It's through my bedroom. Take the first door on the right."

"Thanks. I'll be right back."

"I'll grab our dinner."

"What are we having?" I ask as I walk back into the apartment.

"You'll see."

"More surprises?"

"Of course."

I open the door to Michael's bedroom and it doesn't surprise me to see how neat and tidy it is. I turn on the light and see pictures of him and David on his dresser. My eyes gravitate toward a photo of a younger Michael looking cute in a baseball cap. Then, I pick up one of him and Michelle and laugh at the funny faces they are both making. There's a picture of Michael holding a toddler's hand, and I assume that's his brother. I pick it up and stare into the toddler's wide, brown eyes. Placing the photo back where it belongs, I catch sight of a familiar envelope peeking out from under a newspaper clipping.

My heart freezes, and my hands begin to shake violently as I pick it up and read the headline. "Local 18-Year-Old Deaf Boy and Gas Station Owner Killed in Failed Robbery in Decatur. Suspect Also Shot and Killed."

It can't be. Please.

I read the article and my insides begin to scream uncontrollably. I can't breathe as I place the clipping back on the dresser and pick up the unopened envelope that has my handwriting on it.

"You get lost in here?" Michael asks as he comes into the room and sees me standing with the envelope in my hand, my whole body frozen in place by the frantic sensations zipping through me.

I can barely get the words out. "This is from me, Michael. I wrote this letter."

He stops and stares at me for the longest time. "What are you talking about? How can that be?"

"I was there that night." I hold the letter out. "Here, open it. Please."

He pushes the envelope away.

"Please, Michael," I say, trembling even more as I hold it out to him once again.

"I don't want to read it."

"You have to." I reach out and place the envelope in his hands and then step back.

He opens the letter and begins to read it out loud. Every word, every syllable that he utters causes a fresh wave of tears to streak down my face. I watch in horror as Michael's own tears roll down his cheeks, hitting the brown carpet under his shoes.

"Why didn't you tell me?" he asks through quivering lips.

"I didn't know it was your brother. You never mentioned how he died or when. And the boy that was killed that night was named Daniel Montgomery. Your last name is Davis. How would I have known?"

I search his face, hoping that love and reason are still evident there. But I see neither.

"He was born my cousin. My aunt was a drug addict. She did drugs when she was carrying him, which is why he was born deaf. After she died in childbirth, my mother adopted him. But what does any of that matter now? I want to know why you failed to tell me about this."

"I was scared," I whisper as fear wraps itself around my bones and holds on.

This moment is like a bad dream that I can't seem to wake up from. I feel like I'm fighting for my life, but the reality is that I'm fighting for my future. Our future.

Am I the only one fighting?

Anger sets in behind his eyes, and the sight of it cuts me to the core. My mind races to find the words that will help him understand, help him to forgive, and help me fix this so that I won't lose him.

"My brother is dead, and you're standing here telling me that you were *scared?*"

I take a step toward him, but he ignores my need to be close and moves away instead.

"Michael, please."

"Please? Please, what? Do you think this letter makes it better? Do you think it makes it all just go away?"

He lets go of the letter and the envelope, and we both watch them fall to the carpet next to his tears. When his eyes meet mine again, something inside me somehow understands that the idea of hope is now nothing more than a fantasy.

"You know, every time you talked about Zee, I got jealous. And now I find out that he's the one that took my brother's life." He leans up against his bedroom wall and shoves his hands in his pockets. "I feel…I feel like such a fool."

"I never meant for you to feel that way," I say, desperate to touch him. My heart tells me that if my skin grazes his, even if only for a second, he'll remember the love that he has for me.

I stretch out my hand slowly, but when he stares down at in disbelief, I pull back.

"Zee," he repeats contemptuously, and my heart breaks.

"I always called him Zee, but the name you would have seen on the police report was Zephaniah James Crawford."

"Do you think knowing his full name helps?"

I shake my head and choke back tears. The fire I see in his eyes does not come from love. It comes from somewhere dark, a place that scares me.

"I didn't read that police report after I found out that the store owner killed *Zephaniah* right after a bullet struck and killed my brother," he says, his eyes burning into me. "After that, I didn't want to hear anything else. I had to deal with burying my brother. He was eighteen years old, Mýa. Eighteen!"

"Michael, please know that I tried to stop Zee. I said so in the letter." I bend down to pick the letter up. My hands are shaking, and my heart is beating out of control.

"Leave it down there."

"I'm just trying to explain that I didn't know Zee was going to rob that store until we were sitting out in front of it. He was upset that Mr. Johnson had fired him for stealing. Zee insisted he never stole anything," I say, plucking the letter from the carpet.

"I said leave it down there, Mýa!"

The volume of his voice rips through me and I feel my whole body tremble as I let the letter slip out of my hands and fall to the floor again. Michael turns away from me, and as I stand there feeling hopeless, I hear sobs ripping from his throat.

"Michael, please let me—"

"Comfort me?" he asks, turning back around as tears continue falling down his cheeks. I watch as his body tightens, and his jaw clenches again. *I'm losing him.*

"My brother died so your stupid boyfriend could get some kind of revenge. I don't want your comfort, Mýa."

I take a deep breath. "All I know for certain is that by the time I got out of the car to try and stop him, it was too late."

"You keep saying stuff like that, like it's supposed to make it better. Like your words have some sort of healing power or the ability to just make everything right between us. But here's the thing, Mýa. Right now, they don't." His body sinks down to the carpet and I allow mine to follow.

"Every word is meant to try and bring you back to me. I'm fighting for us. I don't want to lose you. I love you, Michael. Please try to see this from my perspective," I say, reaching out and slowly placing my hand on his.

"What perspective is that?"

"Daniel's death was not my fault. I made a mistake by being with Zee in the first place, and it cost me five years of my life."

"Don't you dare say his name!" he says, pulling his hand away from mine and scrambling to his feet. "I can't even say his name because it hurts too bad. I would give anything to have another five years with him."

"I am not the reason you didn't have those five years, Michael," I say as I slowly stand up.

"But you had a role in taking them away. The woman that I just asked to marry me played a role in my brother's death. You're acting like I'm supposed to be okay with this. Like I'm just supposed to pretend that I forgive you. Tell me, how am I supposed to do that?"

"I don't know. But I do know that we can get through this."

His eyes rest on me, and for a split second I feel hope creeping back into the room.

"Tell me something, Mýa. Would you have ever told me?" he asks. We stand in the center of his bedroom, our bodies tired and weary even as our hearts continue to beat out of control.

"Yes. I was planning on telling you soon. I swear."

He reaches out and touches the side of my chin and I grab his hand to bring it to my lips, kissing it as he stares at me. Begging him with my tears.

"I'm not sure I can get past this, Mýa. I don't know if I can—"

"Forgive me?"

"Yes." He leans over and places his lips on mine, and I pray that he can feel every ounce of love that I have for him in them. But then he abruptly pulls away and steps back. "I think you should go home."

My heart stutters around a beat. It knows that I have lost. It knows that I have lost the fight. "I'll call Jack to come and pick me up," I whisper.

"I'll take you."

"You don't have to do that."

"Yes, I do."

<hr/>

We pull up to my apartment and I reluctantly take the ring off. "Here."

"You keep it."

"I only want to keep it if we're going to be together, Michael."

"I can't promise that right now. Maybe not ever."

"Michael—"

"I'm sorry, Mýa. It may not be right, but I can't help the way I'm feeling right now. I need to leave, and in order to do that, I need you to get out of my car. Please."

I place the ring on his dashboard and then get out of the car.

The worst part about watching him leave is knowing that my heart will always be on Love Lane when it comes to him, but that the two of us would no longer enjoy the ride together.

Tonight is the first night where every page that I write in my journal is filled with tears.

Chapter Forty-five

I sit on Jack and Mary's steps, staring at their door while I debate if I should go in or not. I know they are on the other side, waiting for me to tell them how wonderfully everything went last night. And it had been wonderful—right up to the ugly part.

Then it got really ugly.

Ten minutes go by before Jack opens the door. "Hey, kid, what are you—" He stops when he sees my red and swollen eyes, then sits next to me and takes my hand. "You told him, didn't you?"

All I can do is nod.

"Come on, let's go inside."

"What happened?" Mary asks as Jack closes the door and she gets a good look at me.

"Give her a minute," Jack says as we head to the living room.

"I'll go put on some tea. Whatever it is, Mya, you're going to get through it." Mary places a kiss on my forehead, and my tears begin to fall all over again. Jack and I take a seat on the sofa and wait for Mary to come back into the room. "Tell us what happened while the water is getting hot," she says, easing down into her chair.

I wipe the tears away and start from the joyful beginning, then start to bawl even harder as I get to the end.

"Wow," Jack says as he leans into the sofa and rubs his eyes.

"That's an understatement. I mean, one moment I was cruising down Love Lane, then I was flying down it and making a good right-hand turn on Marriage Lane. And then last night I found myself stalled on Alone Lane."

Mary tries and fails not to laugh. "I'm sorry, but I've never heard it put that way."

"You're right. It sounds ridiculous," I say with a loud sigh. "This is a mess."

Mary stands up. "It's not ridiculous. I'm sorry that I laughed."

"It's okay."

"I'll go and check on the tea."

"Do you have some aspirin? I think I'd rather have just that," I say as I lean back and stare at the ceiling, my brain still trying to process it all.

"Sure, dear. I'll get the aspirin and a cup of water."

Jack places my hand in his again. "You're going to be all right, kid. I promise."

"How, Jack? How am I going to be all right? You weren't there. You didn't see the look on his face, the disappointment, the anger and—dare I say—even a little hatred in his eyes."

"He doesn't hate *you*, just the situation."

"Maybe."

"Mýa."

I stand up. "Don't tell me that I have to keep going. Don't tell me that I can't let this stop me or get me down. Right now, that's all I want. I want to be down. I want to be a mess, and I don't want to pretend like I can get through this without him." I pause and wipe away the tears that threaten to stain my white blouse. "I don't want to lose Michael, but I know that I already have."

"Are you finished?"

"Yes," I say, deflated and feeling like this situation has sucked every ounce of life out of me. And in a sense, it has.

Jack stands up as well. "I was going to tell you to give Michael time. He's not going to come around overnight."

"How much time? Aren't I worth forgiving?"

"Forgiveness is not easy—you should know that. We both knew from the start that Michael wasn't going to start singing 'Happy Days' when he found out."

Mary comes back carrying aspirin and a bottle of water.

"Thank you," I say just as the doorbell rings. I almost fall as I run to the door, wrenching it open and not even registering who's there before I sigh, "Michael."

"Nope, I'm sorry. It's just me," David says.

"Sorry. Come in."

David walks into the front room and shakes hands with Jack and Mary.

"He told you?" I ask.

"He did."

"Of course. How is he?"

"He looks as bad as you do."

"I told her that Michael just needs some time," Jack says.

"And I'm not sure time can heal this one," I say, feeling hopeless.

David sighs as he holds out the black velvet box. "He wants you to keep it. He insists."

"Maybe that's a good sign," I say, clinging to the spark of hope that the box inspires.

David runs his free hand through his hair. "He wants you to keep it because he said he doesn't want anything that reminds him of you."

"I see. I think I need to sit. I didn't think my heart could break any more than it already has, but this takes it to a whole new level."

David hands the black velvet box to Mary. "I'm sorry, Mýa. For the record, I don't feel that he should blame you for Daniel's death, just like I don't blame Michelle for the death of our son. They were both situations that resulted in tragedy, and all of it was beyond your control. From what I read in your letter—"

"He let you read that?" I ask, looking up at him from the sofa.

"He did. I'm sorry. I know it was personal."

"It's okay. Of course Michael let you read it; you're his best friend."

David clears his throat. "From what Michael told me last night, the only person to blame here is Zee. He wanted to rob that store so he could get back at Mr. Johnson for firing him. Zee had that gun, and he intended to use it. There wasn't anything you could have done to stop that."

"That's what I've been trying to tell her for the past four years," Jack says. I shoot Jack a look that begs him to stop talking and he immediately adds, "Sorry, Mýa, but it's true."

"Do you want to stay for dinner?" Mary asks David.

"I wish I could. It smells amazing, but I need to get going. Hang in there, Mýa. I'm on your side."

Jack walks David to the door as I sit and stare at the box in Mary's hand. A strong part of me wants to snatch it out of her hand and fling it across the room.

She must sense that, because Mary puts it down on the sofa and leaves the room.

Chapter Forty-six

I walk into Jack's at five in the morning, hoping no one will notice the bags that are beginning to make a home under my eyes.

"That's two nights in a row with no sleep, kid. You can't continue this way," Jack says as he places a bag of green peppers and some white onions on the counter. "You want an omelet? I can make you one real quick."

I shake my head as I plop down.

"Well, I'm going to make both of us one anyway."

I don't respond as I stare at my coffee cup. I know Jack wants me to go home; he beats a few eggs like they've personally wronged him. But I'm glad he doesn't try to force the issue. I need to be here. I need to be in a place where people love me instead of being at home, staring at a spider that couldn't care less about what I'm going through.

Mary walks in and squeezes my shoulder before making her way to the refrigerator to grab the flowers for the tables.

Maybe you should have stayed home with the spider.

I stand up and put on my apron and name tag.

"Why don't you come and help me put the flowers on the table," she says, rolling the cart filled with flowers in front of me.

"Sure."

"I'll bring the omelets out once they're ready!" Jack shouts as Mary and I head up front.

"You know what you need right now?"

"A very stiff martini?" I say with a sigh as I grab a few flowers and begin inserting them in the vases.

She takes a seat at one of the tables. "Sit."

I walk over slowly and slide into a chair.

"Didn't you tell me that you and your mother used to cook and that you loved it?"

"I did."

"Well, start cooking, and I don't mean with me for our Sunday dinners. Get some cookbooks and start doing something that makes you feel good."

"That would require me having food in my refrigerator. Which I don't."

She laughs. "Well, buy some."

"I could do that," I say as Jack walks over with the omelets that he insisted on making.

"I don't get one?" Mary asks.

He places his omelet in front of her and then turns around and walks back into the kitchen.

"I think I'm going to write him a letter."

Mary doesn't need me to explain who I'm talking about. She simply says, "From what David said, it sounded like you already tried that."

"I know, but I feel like I have some things that I need to say, and since he won't take my calls—" She looks at me sternly, so I add, "Yes, I've tried to call him. Multiple times."

"I guess I would be shocked if you hadn't." She takes a bite of her omelet, and I follow suit. "Okay, get the cookbooks and write Michael the letter."

"Man, this is good," I say as the silence rests between us like an uninvited guest.

"Yeah, mine is very good," Mary says, taking another enthusiastic bite.

"That's because you're eating Jack's."

"Exactly," she says with a sly smile. Then, her expression shifts and she's looking me over with genuine curiosity. "Are you still journaling?"

I place my fork down. "I am. The last few pages are soaked in tears, but the words are there."

"My journal is like my best friend. But don't ever tell Jack that I said that. I'll deny it."

I chuckle, even though there are tears behind my eyes. "Your secret is safe with me."

Chapter Forty-seven

A nother week. Another evening that seems to pass by at a turtle's pace. The only thing that makes this night tolerable is sitting on my new sofa, flipping through a cookbook I picked up at the library. I'm still waiting for my chair to arrive, but the sofa came this afternoon just as I pulled up to my apartment building.

I stop scanning the cookbook and stare at the piece of paper and pen that sits beside me with only two words written on it. *Forgive me.*

Still no calls from Michael.

My stomach growls, so I pick my cookbook back up. Finally, I settle on a creamy garlic Alfredo sauce with bow tie pasta and pan-seared chicken breasts seasoned with rosemary.

It's weird opening my refrigerator and finding food in it. Real food.

I pull out the chicken breasts and begin flattening them out. My phone rings, causing my heart to jump at the thought that it could be Michael. *Please let it be him.*

"Hello," I say softly.

"Is this Mýa Day?"

"It is."

"This is Jazzmyne Mitchell." I almost drop the phone. When I take too long to respond, she adds, "Mýa, you still there?"

"Yes, I'm here," I say, willing my hand to stay steady and my heart to return to a normal pace.

"Did I catch you at a bad time?"

"No, I was just cooking dinner."

"For that overly zealous boyfriend of yours."

I wish. "No, just for me."

"Well, I'm sorry that it's taken me some time to call you, but I was wondering if you could come and see me tomorrow? I'd like to talk to you about performing at my place."

"I work during the day, so it would have to be after I get off."

"Sure, no problem. What's a good time for you? I'll be here all day."

"I work both shifts tomorrow, so how about six?"

"That sounds perfect. I should be able to get away then since my assistant usually gets here around four."

"Great. I'll see you then."

As I place the phone back on the hook, I can't help but let out a little scream of joy. I immediately begin to dial Michael's number after I get myself together, but then I remember our reality. Just like that, the air inside my balloon of joy slowly fizzles out.

Five minutes and a hundred tears later, I call Jack and Mary.

"Hey, kid. What time is it?"

I glance down at my watch. "It's a little after nine. Mary already asleep?" I ask, though I already know the answer.

When you work in a pancake house, getting to bed by eight becomes standard practice. However, after four years, I still haven't adopted the habit. Young and dumb, as Jack would say.

"What's on your mind? Did Michael call or something?"

"No, but I have some good news."

"Good, I could use a little of that to help me get back to sleep."

"Sorry, Jack."

"No worries. Tell me the good news. Sleep is overrated."

"I got a call from that new jazz restaurant you told me about. They want to hire me."

"Congratulations, that is excellent news."

"It feels good to have someone that I can share my news with."

"Well, let me wake Mary up so you will have two people. You know she will want to say congratulations."

I hold while I hear him waking up Mary and telling her what I'd shared with him.

"I'm so excited for you," Mary says. "When do you go see her to get all the details?"

"Tomorrow, after I get off work."

"Aren't you scheduled to work both shifts?" she asks.

"I am, but I told her that I can't come until six."

Jack takes the phone from her. "We can get someone to cover the second shift for you. I want you to have enough time to change out of your uniform and make it over there. You know how bad traffic can be."

"Tomorrow is Saturday, Jack, not a workday. I'll make it with no problem. I'll leave by four, get home by four-thirty, and head back out by five."

"Sounds tight."

"It will work; don't worry."

"Okay, kid. I'm going to close my eyes again, but we'll chat more in the morning," Jack says with a yawn. "I'm happy for you."

"I am, too. I really am."

"You wanted to call Michael and tell him, didn't you?"

"I started dialing his number, but didn't go through with the actual call."

"You know what they say about letting a person go so they—"

"Can come back to you. Yeah, I've heard that. You know what's wrong with that saying, Jack?"

"What?"

"They never say how hard the letting go is."

Chapter Forty-eight

—⁊⁊⁊⁊⁊·

I walk in the door of my apartment at five o'clock. I regret working both shifts, but I'll never tell Jack that. Of course, today of all days, we had to be packed. As in, every seat and a waiting list—packed. I jump in the shower, then frantically search my closet for anything that doesn't require ironing. I settle on the black dress with gold buttons and struggle to put it on while fighting back tears.

For a split second, I seriously consider taking everything off, finding a good Nina Simone song, and drowning myself in a glass of wine. But the thought of Jack's reaction if I have to tell him that I didn't make it tonight is enough to push me out of the house around five thirty.

Thankfully, traffic isn't bad. I reach Jazzmyne's, park, and make it inside with less than five minutes to spare. I spot Jazzmyne standing by the bar and she quickly waves me over.

"Glad to see you made it on time," she says as I fight to catch my breath.

"I can't believe how packed it is in here this early on a Saturday."

"Yes, business has been good, and we intend to keep it that way by providing the best live entertainment and service, and even better food," she proudly says as she scans the crowd. "But enough small talk, let's go back to my office and talk for real—dollars and cents."

"Sounds good."

We walk through the kitchen, and I can't help but notice how impeccably clean it is. Not to say that Jack's kitchen isn't, but I'm sure you can't find even a crumb of food on the floor.

Her office is another story. Papers are everywhere. Boxes have been thrown into every nook and cranny. I'm not sure how Jazzmyne finds anything among all the papers that are piled high on her desk.

Didn't she say that she had an assistant? Maybe she needs two.

I try to smile as she motions toward a chair that I have to clear off before I can even consider sitting down on it.

"Just throw that stuff on the floor. I'm sorry about the mess. I've been busy and haven't had a chance to come in here and get organized. I spend most of my time on the floor, greeting our high-profile guests or performing. That's why I want to hire you; then I can at least take the performing aspect off of my plate."

"You know," I say as I place all the papers that were in the seat on the floor next to me. "I didn't get the impression that you were impressed with my performance."

"In this business, you cultivate a poker face, as they say. I loved your performance. Your boyfriend was right; you can blow."

I settle into my chair. "It doesn't look like Michael still wants to be my boyfriend."

She gives me a commiserative smile. "Sorry to hear that. He seemed like your biggest fan."

"He was." I cross my legs and focus on trying to keep my tears at bay. To steer the conversation away from Michael, I say, "I'm glad to hear that you enjoyed my performance."

"Did you *need* to hear me say that? You should know your skill and have confidence in your own ability," she says, placing her hands on top of her desk and looking me square in the eye. "Frankly, I was a little taken aback by your boyfriend's push that night. It should have come from you. You should have been eager to show the world what you can do. I also found it unimpressive that your then boyfriend had to practically pull you up out of your chair, but I decided to give you the benefit of the doubt. I'm glad I did. I saw that confidence the moment you opened your mouth and introduced your song. You had the audience feeling you before you even pushed out a lyric. That's how this business works. You understand what I mean?"

"I do. I want to sing. It just wasn't always that way for me."

"What changed? If you don't mind me asking."

"Memories of singing in front of my mother and Jack—a man who is like my father that pushed me to come out of my comfort zone."

"Good for him. Or, better yet, good for you."

"Yes, good for me."

"Okay, so here is what I'd like to offer you: four hundred a show. You'll do four shows a week since we're open Thursday through Sunday. It's a one-year contract, but we do provide a W-9, so remember that taxes will come out of that. After a year, we can see where we are."

That's $1600 a week! Is she for real? Please don't let her hear my knees knocking.

"What time would I need to be here?"

"We open the doors at seven on Thursday and Friday and at six on Saturday and Sunday, so you would need to be here by three each day at the latest. This would allow time for you and the band to go over the songs. These guys are professionals. They've done most of the songs played here hundreds of times. We close at eleven."

"Who decides which songs we perform?"

"In the beginning, you and I will meet every Thursday afternoon to make the selections. But, after a month or two, I would like you to run with it. Just keep in mind that we play a wide range of jazz and blues."

"I like that."

"So, we have a deal?"

"We have a deal. When do I start?"

"Next Thursday. I'll have the contract ready for you to sign when you come in. My assistant will help you with the rest of the paperwork. Welcome to Jazzmyne's."

Chapter Forty-nine

"Hey, kid," Jack says as I open the front door of their home and smell the food that Mary has already started cooking. "It smells so good in here. Mary cooking something different?"

"Yeah, she took her own advice and picked up some cookbooks from the library. I think we're having some kind of stuffed fish that I don't know how to pronounce."

"You don't sound thrilled."

"You know I'm not a fancy food kind of man. Give me a steak and some potatoes, or a plate of pasta soaked in a good homemade tomato sauce, and I'm good."

"Well, I can't wait to try it," I say as I plop down on the sofa and Jack takes his usual chair.

He keeps staring at me, so I know that he's waiting for me to tell him about how things went at Jazzmyne's yesterday. Keeping it from him this long is killing me, but it's also so much fun drawing out the suspense. I flip on the television and start surfing channels.

"I thought you would have called us last night and told us how things went," he says after a few minutes. I pretend like I didn't hear him. "Mýa?"

"Yes, Jack?" I force down the grin that wants to make an appearance.

"I know you heard my question," he says, turning the television off.

I laugh, thoroughly enjoying the annoyance on his face. "Okay, you got me. I can't hold it in any longer."

"Hold on," he says before turning his head toward the kitchen. "Mary, get in here. Mýa's got news to share with us." He winks at me. "I thought it better that I tell her this time why I'm shouting."

I wink back. "Good idea."

Mary comes running into the front room with her apron on. "Mýa, I didn't hear you come in. How did it go yesterday? And why didn't you call us last night?"

"I got the gig, and she's paying me four hundred a show! I'll finally be able to afford to buy a home."

"Mýa, that is wonderful!" Mary says.

I look at Jack, waiting for him to say something.

"You're fired."

"What? Wait, Jack—"

"No, Mýa. It's time. I told you that I wouldn't allow you to keep being a waitress, and I meant it."

I look at Mary, hoping that she will jump in here and help plead my case.

"We're going to miss having you there, honey, but it's time," Mary says with tears in her eyes.

"Jack, please give me a few months. The gig is only Thursday through Sunday, and I don't even have to be there until four, so I could still work the breakfast shifts those days." Jack shakes his head. "Okay, then, let me work at the restaurant Monday through Wednesday."

Mary takes a seat. "I just realized this means you won't be able to come for our Sunday dinners anymore."

"Why don't we move them to Monday?" I say. "And you and Jack can come to see me perform on Sundays."

Mary's face lights up. "It won't be quite the same, but it could still work. Jack, what do you think?"

"That's fine. We'll move our Sunday dinners to Monday and hear you perform on Sundays. It will have to be earlier on Sundays; you know we have to get to bed early."

"The place opens at six, so you and Mary can come for the first part of the show and then leave. But what about me working Monday through Wednesday for the first couple of months?"

Jack lets out a long sigh and then smiles. "Three months and breakfast only, starting next week, on Tuesdays and Wednesdays. You need a day off, Mýa."

"Deal," I say.

Chapter Fifty

September 6, 1994

I put my journal down and lean my head against my headboard as I listen to the rain coming down outside. It's soothing and sad. It sounds like the sky is crying. Maybe it's crying for me, shedding the tears that I can't allow to fall as I push through each day without Michael.

I pick my journal back up and carefully tear out a few blank pages from the back.

Dear Michael,

I pray this letter doesn't go unopened. I wish I knew if you were missing me as much as I am missing you.

I can't even look at the black velvet box. It sits on my nightstand, waiting for you to come back and slip the ring on my finger. Please, Michael. Please find it in your heart to forgive me.

You once showed me a picture you took of an older couple kissing on a bridge. You called it Love Endures. But I guess you didn't mean for that to apply to us.

Aren't I worth it? You once said that I was.

Isn't our love strong enough to get through this? Strong enough to help us find a way to see our future together?

Since that night, that fateful night, I've come to realize how much I needed to forgive myself. How much I needed to let go of the past. I learned that the past couldn't keep me warm at night.

Real love doesn't come often. Some never touch it. But we did. We wrapped ourselves in it.

Real love has an aroma. Some never get to smell its beautiful scent. But we bathed in it.

I could go on and on describing real love, but all I have to do is think about you and what we shared—the way you made me feel.

So now I ask you to think about me. The way I made you feel.

Come back to me.

Love,

Mýa

Chapter Fifty-one

—{{{{{•

My life is changing. It's a hard reality for me to grasp. Knowing that this detour is good for me should make it easier for me to wrap my head around, but it doesn't. I feel strange walking into Jack's and knowing that for the next three months, I'll only be here two days a week, and then that's the end. A four-year journey has brought me to this point, but now it's closing. It's even harder for me to accept that this exciting new chapter in my life is being written without Michael.

I keep telling myself to snap out it. To accept it. To find happiness in myself and let go of the things that I have no control over. Like Michael's decision to walk away from us.

From me.

"Fall is coming in soon," Jack says as he begins taking the chairs off the tables in preparation for the breakfast crowd.

"Just a couple of weeks away," I say, putting my purse down so I can help him. I can tell there's something on his mind. "Everything okay, Jack? You look deep in thought, and you were pretty quiet at dinner last night."

"Nothing is wrong, kid. You decide where you're going to buy your house?"

"It's all still too new. I'll wait until after I've signed that contract on Thursday and have been working there a good six months before I even consider it." I wait for him to tell me to go for it now, but he doesn't say anything.

It's almost silent when Mary comes up front with the flowers and starts putting them in the vases. Finally, I can't take the awkwardness anymore.

"What's going on here?" I demand.

Mary looks up. "Nothing. Why?"

"You two are never this quiet."

"Jack has a doctor's appointment today. You know how he gets when he has to see the doctor. He'll never admit it, but I think he's afraid of needles."

The simple explanation makes me feel a bit better, and my shoulders relax. "I don't blame him. I can't stand them, either."

"He'll be back to his normal grumpy self once it's all over."

"I can hear both of you," Jack says. Mary and I look at each other and grin.

"By the way," she says to me. "Jack's nephew is coming by the house tonight. Why don't you come over, too? We might as well start having our family dinners on Mondays now."

"Sounds good. I've never met Jack's nephew before."

"That's because he lives in New York. He moved out there to study under some well-known chef. We haven't seen Matt for thirteen—no, fifteen years."

"That's a long time. Is he here for good or just visiting?"

Mary glances over at Jack. "He's here for business. It will be so nice to see him. He was such a quirky kid, but boy, could he cook."

"He's a spoiled kid who doesn't appreciate the family business, is what he is," Jack says as he storms into the kitchen.

"Wow. Now I know exactly how Jack really feels about him."

"Don't pay Jack any mind. Matt helped Jack here all through high school, but once he graduated, he left. Jack hasn't forgiven him."

"Jack's the most forgiving man I know, so there has to be more to the story."

Mary edges closer to me, lowering her voice. "Jack will never tell anyone this, but he pleaded with Matt to stay. He loved having him in the kitchen with him. You should have seen the two of them. When Matt decided to go to New York, he and Jack got into a nasty argument, and some hurtful words came out of both of them. Matt told Jack that making pancakes was not real cooking, and that he wanted to be trained by a real chef."

"Ouch. I can see why Jack is still hurt."

"Yeah. They haven't spoken since. But I'm hoping that tonight they can find a way to forgive each other. It's been long enough."

"Apparently not, according to Jack," I say.

"Jack knows what he has to do. He'll do the right thing."

"I hope so. You know how stubborn Jack can be."

"I'm not worried about Jack's stubbornness. What needs to happen will happen," Mary says as we head into the kitchen.

Chapter Fifty-two

I arrive at Jack and Mary's house wearing jeans and a blue floral shirt.

"Looks like you finally washed your clothes," Mary says, glancing my way as she covers a couple of thinly sliced chicken breasts with olive oil.

"I know, right? It feels good to finally get back into my jeans. Dresses and skirts were starting to take over my life. Where's Jack?"

"He's in the bedroom, lying down."

"He okay?"

"He's fine. Just a little tired from his doctor's visit. You know how those physicals can wear a person out."

"It's hard to imagine Jack getting worn out."

"We all have our limitations. Sometimes it just takes some of us longer to accept them."

"So true." I had a feeling she was speaking more about me than Jack.

"Nothing from Michael yet?" Mary says suddenly, turning the oven on. "Did you send him the letter?" she asks as she moves toward the counter and folds her hands on top of it.

I pull a stool out from under the counter and take a seat. "Not a sound from him, but yes, I finally sent him the letter. I imagine that, by now, it's probably sitting on his dresser, unopened, or in the trash."

She frowns and then glances back at the oven to check if the warming light has gone off or not. "He just needs time."

I rest my hands on top of the counter as well. "That's what everyone keeps telling me. It's been weeks. I'm starting to wonder if Michael loved me as much as he said he did."

A crease forms on her forehead. "I don't think that's a fair assessment to make," Mary says as she makes her way back over to the oven and then places the chicken inside. "It's not like the situation is an easy one. It was his brother, after all."

"I know. I just miss Michael so much." I can't help but feel like a little girl pouting because she can't have something she wants.

"Mýa, I think you might have to prepare yourself for the worst. Michael may not ever be able to forgive you. I'm sorry. I know that sounds harsh, but you need to hear it."

I frown, but I know she's right. "It's not harsh. I've thought a lot about that possible reality. If it wasn't for journaling every night, I don't think I would be able to stop crying."

"Journaling helps."

"It sure does. But enough about my dead love life. Where's the quirky nephew?" I ask as Mary starts making a mushroom cream sauce for the chicken.

"I'm right here," he says, placing his cell phone in his pocket as he walks into the kitchen wearing a pair of jeans and a white shirt. I take in his round blue eyes, curly brownish-blond hair, and nicely toned build. Our eyes meet and linger for a second or two before he focuses back on his aunt. "Sorry, Mary. That call took longer than I expected."

"Everything okay?" she asks him as I look away.

"Yes, everything is fine. I just wanted to see if the airline found my clothes yet," he says.

"What did they say?"

"They haven't, so it looks like I'm going to have to go and buy this quirky boy some new clothes." He glances my way and winks.

I clear my throat. "I'm sorry, I was just—"

"Don't worry about it," he says with a grin. "I was a quirky kid when I was younger, but I think I've grown out of that now, don't you think?"

He's got the confidence thing down pat.

I feel myself blushing as my eyes roam his face and watch the movement of his throat when he swallows.

"Of course you have. You've become a handsome young man," Mary says with a slight grin, having caught me watching him as he walks over to taste her sauce. "Matt, did you say hello to Mýa?"

He gives me a smirk. "So you're Mýa. I've heard nothing but good things about you. According to Mary, you're more like their daughter than a friend of the family."

I feel his eyes taking me in, too, from my heels resting on the counter to the red lipstick that I decided to wear today. "Jack and Mary are my family," I finally say.

"Well then, I guess that means we're related. But I'm glad it's not by blood," he says with a smile that shows off a dimple in his left cheek that mimics Jack's.

I hope he's not trying to flirt with me.

I hand him an apple out of the basket on the counter. "Peace offering."

He smiles again as he takes the apple. I can't help but notice that his dimple grows even deeper as he takes a bite out of it. "Thanks."

"Again, I'm sorry about the 'quirky' comment," I say, still trying to redeem myself.

"No worries, really." He looks over at Mary as he takes another bite from the apple and I force myself to focus on something other than him. "That sauce is good," he continues. "Throw some fresh garlic and butter in there for some serious pop. Where's my Uncle Jack? Still asleep?"

"Great idea," Mary says as she turns to the refrigerator to grab them both. "Jack will be up in a few. You and Mýa can go ahead and set the table for me. Everything is there on counter next to her."

"Sure," Matt says. As he makes his way over, I get a faint whiff of his cologne. "Do you cook, Mýa?"

"Mýa is a great cook. Her mother taught her," Mary says as Matt grabs the plates and I stand to pick up the silverware and the glasses.

I look over at Mary suspiciously, and she pretends she suddenly needs to grab something out of the refrigerator.

"I love to cook. I just recently started dabbling with recipes after Mary encouraged me."

"Bad breakup, huh?"

I'm going to kill Mary. "We're not broken up—just trying to work some things out, that's all. It's complicated."

"Most breakups are complicated," Matt says as we enter the dining room.

"Again, we're not broken up."

"But he told you that you could keep the ring, right?"

I put the silverware and the cups on the table with perhaps a little more force than is necessary. "Okay, so how much of my love life did Mary tell you about?"

He grins. "I got here early this morning, and we've been chatting since they came back from the doctor. So probably all of it."

"Great," I say, thoroughly embarrassed and slightly irritated at Mary for telling him my business.

"It's okay. I just went through something similar."

"I doubt it."

"At least you said yes when he asked."

"Oh. Sorry," I say with a wince. "I'm sure that was tough."

"Her name is Laura. She's one of the sous chefs at the restaurant I worked for."

"Ouch," I say as I pull out the nicer placemats that Mary keeps in the china cabinet and arrange them on the table so that Matt can put the plates down.

"'Ouch' is right. In the end, things took a pretty ugly turn—what with me being the head chef and all."

"So, is that why you're here? To get away from it all?"

"Maybe, but mainly because there are some important things here that need my help."

"Important things? Like what?" I ask out of sheer curiosity.

"Just family stuff."

"Oh, I see."

Now it's Matt's turn to wince. "Sorry, I didn't mean that the way it might have sounded. I know you're a part of this family."

"It's okay. I understood what you meant."

"Thanks, I appreciate that. Anyway, I figure my coming gives me a chance to make amends with Uncle Jack. I'm sure Mary told you the story of how I became the black sheep of the family."

"Black sheep?"

His face turns the color of a beet. "I keep putting my foot in my mouth, don't I? Again, I didn't mean that the way it came out."

"Got you back," I say with a smirk.

"Funny. I like a woman with a good sense of humor."

Our eyes meet in the middle of the table, but I look away.

Okay. Yes, he's flirting with me.

"Glad to see you two getting along so well," Jack says as he comes into the dining room.

Matt's shoulders tense up, but he offers his hand to Jack anyway. "Uncle Jack, it's good to see you."

Jack looks down at Matt's extended hand, but refuses to take it. "It's been fifteen years, and you think we're just going to shake hands like all is well between us?"

"Uncle Jack, can't we let the past stay in the past?"

"You thought you were better than me!" Jack lets his hand fall flat on the table, rattling the glasses.

Mary walks into the dining room with her dish gripped firmly between two oven mitts. "That's enough, Jack. Everyone take a seat, please. We're going to have dinner like the grown-ups I know we are." She glares at Jack. "Right?"

"I'm not making any promises," he grumbles.

"It smells good, Mary. I can't wait to taste it," I say, hoping to lighten the mood as we sit down to eat.

This is my first time experiencing complete silence at Jack and Mary's table.

"That was good, Mary," Jack says as he reaches over and squeezes her hand.

"Why don't we put some music on while we eat dessert?" I say, trying to dispel the frosty air that seems to be lingering from Jack and Matt's earlier spat.

"I hear music and pie go well together," Matt chimes in.

"They do, don't they?" I say, thankful that he's willing to play along.

"Are you going to sing for us after we're done, Mýa?" Matt asks.

I look at Mary, who starts to fidget in her seat. "I only told him because I am so proud of you."

I sigh and then smile at her. "I know. It's okay."

"But I forgot to tell him that you just landed a gig at a new jazz restaurant near Perimeter Mall, so you'll only be working at Jack's a couple of days now." Mary leans back in her chair. "There, I think he's completely caught up now."

I shake my head and reach for a piece of pie. I can't even get upset with her; we've already had enough of that going on tonight.

"Congratulations. So, am I going to get to hear your amazing voice tonight?" Matt asks again.

"Not tonight." I say as a hint of disappointment shows in his eyes. "Maybe at the next Monday night family dinner. If you're still here then, of course."

"Matt is moving back here," Mary says abruptly.

I shoot Mary a quick look.

I've never seen her like this. She must be trying to fill in Jack's part of the conversation. "Really?" I ask Matt. "You're leaving your position as head chef at some fancy restaurant in New York to move back to Atlanta?"

He places his hands on top of the table and nods. "I am. I bought a condo here. I close on it tomorrow. I'm nervous because I haven't seen it yet."

"That was dumb," Jack says.

Mary shoots him a disapproving look as he reaches over to grab a slice of pie.

"You must have had a great real estate agent to convince you to buy it without taking a tour," I say, ignoring Jack's comment.

"I did. My agent did a wonderful job. She took plenty of pictures, and

I had it inspected by the best to ensure there weren't any hidden issues. The condo is only six years old, so they didn't find much, and the current homeowners agreed to fix the minor things."

"Nice. Where is it?"

"Mýa wants to buy a house," Mary offered as an aside.

"Mary," I snap.

"Sorry," she says.

Jack smiles. It's the first time he's done so all evening.

"It's near downtown and within walking distance to most of the shops and restaurants," Matt answers without missing a beat.

"Sounds amazing," I say, grabbing another slice of pie to wrap up and take home with me. "What are you going to do about work? Did you find something already?"

"I have a prospect, but there are a few things that need to be worked out. You know how that goes. If you're still looking for a house, I'd be happy to give you my real estate agent's contact information. As I said, she did a wonderful job for me. I highly recommend her."

"I have—sure, actually. That would be great. Although I probably won't be in the market for at least another six months or so."

"Okay. I'll be sure to give it to you before you leave tonight. I might forget to do it later, so just remind me if I do. When do you start your new gig?"

"I start on Thursday. I'm nervous."

"Don't be," Jack says, finally joining in on our conversation for more than a snarky comment here and there. "She hired you because you can sing, and better than these so-called singers out there doing all that talking instead of actually singing like they're getting paid to do."

Matt looks over at me with an arched brow.

"Jack's not a fan of rap," I explain.

"I don't blame him," Mary says with a glance over at Jack, clearly glad to have him back. "I can't figure out what they're actually saying, but I will admit that I like the beat in some of it."

"Do you like rap?" Matt asks me as he places his napkin down on the table and eases back in his chair.

"Not really, but I do respect that some rappers use it as a way to express how they feel about things that have happened in their lives. I'd compare some of it—not all of it, mind—to spoken word."

"Good point," Matt says. "Rap isn't my favorite, but it's becoming a prominent form of expression these days. I prefer singers like Aretha Franklin, Whitney Houston, and Celine Dion. I'm also a huge jazz enthusiast. Billie Holiday is one of my favorites."

He listens to Billie Holiday?

"On that note, let's listen to some music," Mary says.

Chapter Fifty-three

—*{{{{{{*•

September 22, 1994

Thursday arrives like it has business to take care of. I pull into the parking lot of Jazzmyne's wearing a floor-length, cuff sleeve black gown that Mary purchased for me. She called it her apology. I call it absolutely beautiful. The gold stud earrings and black satin flats that I picked up at Macy's have me feeling extra special as I find a parking spot.

Mary had clapped when I told her that for tonight, I'd be replacing my ninety nine cent lipstick with the grown woman kind and splurging on a gold eye shadow that promises to stay on my eyelids forever. Or hopefully for at least the next eight hours or so.

Glancing in the rearview mirror of my car, I smile. My hair is starting to grow in more and I can finally see a deeper wave pattern. I put enough mousse and gel in it today to ensure it's visible to everyone else, too. I check my watch and see that I'm fifteen minutes early.

Fifteen minutes to sit and think about how the first time I came here, I had been with Michael.

Don't cry. Tonight is not the night for that foolishness.

Too late.

—*{{{{{{*•

"Hi," says a young woman with brown skin, braces, and long hair. "You must be our new singer? I'm Margaret."

"Nice to meet you, Margaret. I assume you're Jazzmyne's assistant?"

"Sorry, I should have explained that part, too. It's been a busy day and it's only four. Come on, let's get your paperwork done. I have everything ready for you to sign. Once we're finished, I'll introduce you to the band and let you take it from there. They are eager to see what songs you've selected for tonight's show."

My eyebrow lifts. "I guess Jazzmyne isn't going to be here to assist me with that like she and I discussed?"

She smirks. "One thing you'll learn fast here is that Jazzmyne promises to be a lot of places and rarely shows up at any of them. I'm surprised she was actually there to go over the offer of employment with you. Typically, I handle that as well."

"So you're more like a manager than her assistant?"

"Now you're getting it. You'll love her, though. Flaws and all, she cares about everyone that works for her."

"I could see that about her."

"Follow me. I promise we'll get this done quickly so you can have time to put a list together before meeting the band."

"Thank you."

"No problem. By the way, I love your dress. Very elegant and perfect for the stage. Jazzmyne always knows who to hire. I can tell she was spot-on with you."

I can tell that Margaret is a talker. "Thank you," I say as I follow her to the smaller office located next to Jazzmyne's. It's as neat as the kitchen here is.

She notices me taking a look around. "Neat and organized, huh?"

I smile. "Yes."

We both laugh and then she pulls out the paperwork, which I sign in less than ten minutes.

———

As I stand in front of the band, going over the songs that I selected, I pray they can't hear my knees knocking under my dress.

"I'm digging your choices for tonight," Jim, the bass player, says to me. *Digging? That's some real old-school talk.*

"Thank you," I say. "I really wish I had come earlier so we could all take some time to get to know each other. Jazzmyne told me to be here at four."

"Don't worry about it. We all heard you sing. Anyone that can blow like that, we'll follow. No worries."

"I appreciate that."

"By the way, that cat sitting behind the drums is Malcolm. Don't mind the tattoos running down his arms and hands. He looks scary, but he's as gentle as a kitten. Your other guitarist is my twin brother Kenny. He's shy, so don't expect him to say much, but he'll tear up that guitar for you. I promise you that. Tommy is your master on the keys. That white boy can play a piano like his mama slapped some soul in him. You'll see."

I laugh at that one and give each of the band members a polite nod.

"I'm glad I finally got you to relax. Like I said, we'll have your back and you don't have to worry, we're all married, so there won't be any flirting going on. We're all about the music and nothing else."

"That's good to know," I say, feeling even more awkward now. "Maybe we should get rehearsal started?"

"Which one do you want to start with?" he asks.

I look over my list. "Let's start with a little Minnie Riperton."

"Dig that."

Jazzmyne takes the stage at exactly seven o'clock wearing a long cream dress and silver earrings.

"Impressive, isn't she?" Margaret says as we come to the right of the stage.

She is, considering she just walked in five minutes ago.

"That's our Jazzmyne. You'll go on when she's done giving her typical 'welcome to Jazzmyne's' speech. I'm sure you heard it when you came the first time?"

"I did," I say, trying not to seem nervous. The rapid beating of my heart is telling a different story.

"Have a great show. I have to go and check on the bar."

I take a deep breath as Jazzmyne finishes up, then I walk out on the stage and gently wrap my hands around the microphone. "Good evening. We're going to start this evening off with my second favorite singer, Minnie Riperton," I say to the audience just as I spot Jack, Mary, and even Matt staring back up at me.

I begin to sing the first set of lyrics, and my eyes automatically search the dimly lit space for him.

For Michael.

Chapter Fifty-four

November 29, 1994

"I'm so glad to see the sun out today," I say as I grab a spoonful of eggs off the grill and dump them on top of my toast. "We need the heat."

"I agree. That sun felt good on my bones this morning," Mary says. We both watch Matt slice up a bowl of mushrooms quicker than I have ever seen anyone do it, including Jack.

"It's also been good seeing the tension between Jack and Matt starting to lift," I say to Mary, keeping my voice low enough that Matt doesn't overhear.

"It only took a couple of months—way too long in my book," Mary says, moving closer to me.

"You know how stubborn your husband is," I say with a smirk, placing my hands on my hips.

"All too well, but like I told you before, Jack knew what had to be done."

"You did tell me that," I say, allowing my hands to drop. I look Matt's way again and admire the way he coaches another cook on how to prepare one of four new sauces that Jack allowed him to add to the menu. "You think Matt's going to stay?"

"Matt isn't going anywhere," she says, confidently.

"How can you be so sure?"

"He's where his heart wants to be," she says, giving me a pinch.

"What's that supposed to mean?"

"Only that this is home for him now."

I nod. "Jack certainly seems to think so. Matt is practically running the kitchen for him."

"It's what Jack always wanted. It just took him a minute to remember that."

"Speaking of Jack," I say. "I hope his stomach starts feeling better. It's weird being here and not seeing him, and he went to bed right after we finished dinner yesterday."

"He says it's all the fancy food I've been cooking lately. He'll be here tomorrow, just as grumpy as ever. Don't worry."

I laugh. "That's Jack," I say as I slip my apron on, then pause and debate whether now is a good time for us to talk. Making up my mind, I ask, "Mary, before we open, I wanted to chat with you for a few minutes. Can we go back to the office?"

"Sure. I'll be back there in a minute; just let me get the last few flowers out on the tables."

"You want me to help you?"

"No, finish up your sandwich. It's only a few."

As I take the last few bites of my egg sandwich, I glance up and see Matt looking my way.

"You want some more eggs?" he asks.

"No thanks. They were amazing, though. Thanks for fixing them for me. Did you do something different to them than what we serve to the customers?" I ask.

He walks over from behind the grill, and as I breathe in his cologne, I feel a tingle in my toes. *What's up with you, girl?*

"I used my secret spice recipe."

"You're going to have to give that to me."

"It's going to cost you," he says with a smile that reaches his eyes.

"Cost me what?"

Mary walks back into the kitchen before he can respond. "You still need me, Mýa?"

I clear my throat and try to hide my embarrassment. "I do."

"All right, let's go back."

I look back at Matt as I follow her to the office and see that he hasn't taken his smiling eyes off me.

Really girl, what are you doing?

"Okay, tell me what's wrong," Mary says, closing the door as I take a seat in front of Jack's desk. She eases down in the chair next to me rather than taking the one her husband normally occupies.

"How do you know something is wrong?" She gives me the side-eye and I immediately cave. "Right. I ran into David last night."

"Where?"

"At the gas station down from your house, believe it or not."

"Of course. What was he doing downtown?"

"Picking up some special wine for his sister, Jenna. She's living here now and staying with him until she can find a place of her own. David said the cold weather in Chicago finally got to her."

I can feel Mary studying my facial expressions as I talk. "So, how is David doing?"

"He was smiling, so that was a good thing. We spoke briefly about my gig at Jazzmyne's and he shared how things are going for him. He said he's still not sleeping that much."

"I remember those sleepless nights. The ceiling becomes your best friend."

"That's what he said." I grow silent for a second, knowing she's waiting for me to tell her if I asked David about Michael. Finally, I blurt out, "Yes, I asked him if Michael talks about me."

"And?"

"According to David, he doesn't."

"How do you feel about that?"

"It didn't hurt as deeply as I thought it would. Don't get me wrong, it stung, but it didn't feel like a knife was cutting into me."

She places her hands in her lap. "That means your heart is healing."

"Maybe. At least the tears have stopped."

"Do you think you're going to give him the ring back?"

"I am. Or I guess I should say I *will*. He should have it, since it's obvious we're not getting back together."

She reaches over and squeezes my hand. "Do you think you can face him?"

I shake my head. "I'm going to mail it to him. David told me rather frankly that Michael doesn't care to see me."

"I'm so sorry," Mary says as she places her hands back in her lap. "I know hearing that wasn't easy."

I give her a wry smile and shrug my shoulders. "It wasn't, but it's okay. As far as I'm concerned, it is what it is. I've done all I can. I finally stopped searching the audience after every show at Jazzmyne's for him. My heart got tired of breaking."

Mary shakes her head firmly. "No, your heart told you that it's time to move on."

"I guess you're right. Can I ask you something, though? Something very personal about you and Jack?"

"Okay," she says, leaning back slightly in her chair.

"When Jack met you, do you think he was over *her*? His ex-girlfriend, the one that—"

"I know who you are referring to," she says matter-of-factly.

"Sorry, you don't have to answer that if you don't want to."

She takes a minute, allowing my question to roll around in the air between us. "I will say this—your first love is *always* your first love. You never really forget them, but they stop occupying so much of your mind. They stop taking up all the space in your heart because it eventually makes room for someone or something else. In time, even the little bit of room that seemed to hang on for them gets filled up, and you find yourself loving completely again."

"That's how it happened for Jack."

She smiles. "That's how it will happen for you, too. I promise."

"Maybe your heart feels a tingle at first?" She gives me a confused look, so I say, "Never mind. Thanks, Mary. I really needed this *girl talk*, as Jack would call it if he were here today."

"Yep, Jack would call it just that."

Chapter Fifty-five

—⟨⟨⟨⟨⟨⟨•

December 12, 1994

"Hi, Matt," I say, walking into the kitchen at Jack and Mary's house. "Man, it's cold out there."

"They said we might see a few flurries of snow as early as next week."

"It rarely snows here. I bet you miss that about New York."

"The snow? Absolutely not. Although it was pretty to look at."

"I'm sure," I say, taking off my coat. "Whatever you're cooking over there smells incredible."

"It's my homemade marinara sauce. Come and taste it," he says, dipping a wooden spoon into the pot.

"Wow, that's beyond incredible. It's so smooth and full of flavor. The garlic and the tomatoes just pop in your mouth."

He grins. "Glad you like it."

"Not to get dramatic on you, but that is the best marinara sauce I have ever tasted. I bet people are missing your cooking in New York."

"There are a lot of great chefs in New York; I was just one of them. Besides, this is my home now," he says, looking directly at me.

Don't blush, and definitely don't keep looking him in the eyes.

I glance over and see the pasta maker. "Don't tell me you made that pasta by hand?"

"I did. It's not that hard once you get used to doing it, and it makes the sauce taste so much better. An Italian chef taught me."

"You're going to have to show me how to make it."

"I'd love to. Why don't you come by my place next Wednesday around six? Bring your apron."

"Yes, chef," I say jokingly.

We're both still laughing as Mary walks into the kitchen.

"It sure is nice to have someone else preparing dinner," she says.

"You know I love to cook," Matt says, giving his sauce another stir.

"This kitchen smells like one of those fine dining restaurants," Jack says as he joins us and takes a seat at the kitchen table.

"Jack, you look tired," I say. "Was it busy at the restaurant today? I miss being there on Mondays."

"Get used to it," he says with a smirk. "Actually, in another week, you won't be working there at all. We said three months, and the end of next week will be the three-month mark."

"Stop reminding me, Jack."

He just winks at me.

"I've been meaning to tell you how much I enjoy hearing you sing, Mýa. You have an amazing talent, but I'm actually more impressed with how skillfully you handle the crowd," Matt says. "You can tell they love the way you tell a story about each song before it's performed."

"Thanks. I started adding that in on a whim, and everyone seems to enjoy it."

"When I was young, Jack used to tell me that anyone can learn to cook. But when your food tells a story, people know that you're not just a good cook, but a cook that cares."

I look over at Jack. "Is that a tear I see?"

"Of course not," he says as he pretends there's something in his eye.

"Matt, I can't believe you've come with Jack and Mary every Sunday."

"I wouldn't want to be anywhere else," he says, looking directly at me in that intense way of his again.

Out of the corner of my eye, I see Mary staring at us.

"Is the food ready?" Jack asks when I finally manage to look away.

Matt gives his sauce a quick taste. "It's ready," he says, but I can still feel his eyes on my skin.

"Good, because I'm ready to eat," Jack says as stands and then heads to the dining room table.

"I guess that's our cue to get this dinner started," Matt says. "You guys go on. I'll make up the plates and bring them to the table."

"I'll help," I say.

"Even better. Why don't you add the pasta, and I'll add the sauce?"

"Sounds like a plan," I say, jumping up and grabbing the first plate. We both reach for the spoon, and Matt rests his hand on top of mine. "I don't know why I was reaching for a spoon to add the pasta. Sorry about that."

"I'm not."

I feel like he's looking into the core of my soul with those deep blue eyes as I move around him to get to the drawer that holds Mary's pasta server. She comes back into the kitchen, takes one look at us, and turns back around.

"That was awkward," I say. "I have a feeling Mary thinks something is happening between us."

"I would like that," he admits, breaching the small space that's between us. "But I know you're still getting over Michael."

"Aren't you still trying to get over Laura?"

"I closed that chapter of my life the moment I realized I wanted to start a new one with you."

"I have a past," I say abruptly. There's no sense keeping it quiet, especially considering what happened the last time I waited to tell someone I really cared about.

"I know all about your past, and I don't care about it. Give me a chance, Mýa." He reaches out and runs his fingers along the underside of my chin. The intimate gesture causes my heart to step out of the darkness that it's been in.

"I don't know if I can go there again with someone else," I whisper.

"We'll take things slow. No expectations. Let's just see where it leads us. Promise me that you'll at least think about it."

"I promise," I say, stepping back but knowing in my kidneys that the connection between us has already taken root.

We finish filling the plates and carry them to the dining room.

Chapter Fifty-six

I step into the elevator wearing a pair of black jeans, boots, and a cream sweater under my coat. Pushing the button for the tenth floor, I lean up against the wall, unsure why I'm so nervous.

He's just teaching you how to make pasta. It's not a date.

The moment I walk into Matt's apartment, I hear Michael Bolton singing "All for Love." I know I'm in trouble the second I see him standing there looking like a tall glass of crisp and refreshing white zinfandel, and that I want precisely that—a date, and more.

"Glad you made it," he says as he takes my coat.

"Sorry I'm a little late. I couldn't find my car keys."

"No worries. I've lost mine plenty of times. Are you ready?"

I open my purse and pull out my apron. "All set," I say as I slip it on.

Matt walks around and ties it from the back for me. His hands linger on my waist for a second and I welcome the touch.

"I like the perfume you're wearing," he murmurs.

"Thanks," I say, feeling the warmth of his hands through my sweater. "I like how open your place is. You can see the kitchen from pretty much any angle, and your view is simply breathtaking. All of downtown appears to be out there." I step away and move toward his big bay windows.

"Yeah, I love that view, too. When the real estate agent showed me the photos, I didn't care about much else." He walks into the kitchen and pours both of us a glass of wine, then hands me one. "For you."

I take a sip. "This is nice. It has a subtle sweetness to it."

"It does. If you really like it, we can always go to a wine tasting sometime. They're having one at this venue called Marla's Vino on the second Saturday in January. I believe it starts at one, and it's only thirty minutes from Jazzmyne's. We could grab some lunch at one of the restaurants nearby before the tasting starts. We'd be done by two at the latest. I know you have to be at work by four."

"Sounds like you've given this some thought," I say with a small grin.

"I was hoping we could spend more time together besides Monday dinners at Jack and Mary's house or on Sundays, when I only get to see you on stage. Especially now that you're no longer working at the restaurant."

"I'd like that."

"Really?" he asks, placing his glass of wine down on the counter and moving into my space. Our eyes dance, and the sight blocks out the world that's still turning around us. "Which part would you like? Going to the wine tasting, or spending more time together?"

"All of it," I whisper as his lips come within inches of my own.

He's about to kiss you.

His lips softly brush mine and linger as I rest my hands on his waist.

"I've been waiting to do that for months now. Every time you came in for work at Jack's, I had to fight the urge to pull you out back."

I let out a small laugh. "Really?"

"Really," he says, tilting my head back slightly as I rise up on my toes so I can feel his lips on mine again. The way our bodies touch makes me feel like they've always been this way, like Matt has always been in this space.

"You're supposed to be showing me how to make pasta," I say after I catch my breath.

"Right," he says, taking a quick sip of his wine. Then another one. "Okay, let's get started."

———·{{{{{·

After dinner, we nestle down on the floor in front of his sofa and enjoy the view, chatting about what seems like everything while Billie Holiday plays in the background. I watch his mouth move in the flickering light of two candles, which blends nicely with the moonlight streaming into his apartment.

There's something about Matt. Something comforting. Listening to his voice makes me feel like I've known him my whole life. Maybe that's because we already know each other and I don't feel like my past is sitting between us, creating a barrier that I'm afraid to climb over or get around.

As the light dances in his eyes, I feel myself not caring what it is.

Chapter Fifty-seven

February 1, 1995

I rush around my apartment, checking my watch every ten minutes or so as I eagerly wait for Matt to show up.

I'm glad the landlord gave me the okay to paint the walls gray and give the trim around my apartment a good coat of winter white. Every now and then, I find myself stopping to stare at the dark wood table with matching chairs that's giving my kitchen a modern flair. The gray and white rug that Mary purchased gives my sofa and chair more style, and the few pieces of art that I found at a secondhand store add just the right pop of color to the space.

Of course, Jack almost lost his mind when I pulled more money out of my savings to do all of this, but once he saw my apartment's transformation, he agreed it was long overdue. Thanks to him, I now have a color television with a remote.

I hear the timer that I set for my roast as Matt walks in, wearing jeans and a navy-blue sweater. "Smells good."

"Where's your coat?" I ask as I pull the roast out of the oven.

"It's not that cold out there."

"It's the middle of February, so yes, it's cold."

"Cold is what New York is around this time. That's when I wear a coat."

"Fair enough," I say as he walks over and kisses me.

"I haven't had a roast in a long time," he says, glancing down at mine. "I love all the vegetables you have placed around it."

"I hope you like it."

"It smells too good for it to taste bad, but anything is possible," he says, pulling me in for another kiss.

"Stop that before my roast gets cold," I say, separating from him.

"I don't mind a cold roast. It makes a great sandwich."

"Well, I do mind, and I'm hungry."

"Okay, I'll give your lips a rest so they can get some food."

"Thank you. I appreciate that."

"*My* lips don't."

"Why don't you pour us a glass of wine, and I'll start the salad?"

I watch as he moves around my apartment like he's been in it a hundred times. And at this point, that isn't far from the truth. Matt and I spend every Tuesday and Wednesday either at his apartment or mine, and that's if we aren't going out. Mondays, of course, we spend with Jack and Mary. And of course, he still comes to every Sunday show at Jazzmyne's with his aunt and uncle. Although, for the last couple of Sundays, Jack hasn't been looking very well.

"Matt, do you think something is wrong with Jack?"

"Why?"

"I don't know. It just seems like he's been moving around gingerly lately, and he always seems to be tired."

"Business at the restaurant has been crazy. We've even brought in more staff to help us keep up."

"I know. But all of that business is a direct result of your new sauces and the other additions you've made to the menu. I'm so proud of you."

"I wish I could convince Jack to open for dinner."

"Keep working on him. Jack knows what needs to happen. He'll agree to it, I'm sure."

"Mary told me something similar when she and I discussed it," he says as we fix our plates and move to the kitchen table.

"Well, you know Mary knows him better than either one of us, so if she thinks he'll start opening up to it, then you can consider it done."

He laughs. "You're right."

"Speaking of making some changes, I might be making a few of my own," I say as I pour each of us a glass of wine. "I was talking to Jazzmyne earlier today. She called me to see if I would be interested in recording something with the band. Apparently she has a record label that wants to talk to me."

"Is that what you want?" he asks as he takes a sip of wine.

"I don't know. It's a thought."

"Well, if that's something you decide to do, I'll support you."

"I know you will, and I thank you for that."

As I watch Matt eat his salad, I can't help but smile. I like that he understands that it has to be my decision, that he doesn't push or try to convince me to do anything. I reach over and wrap my hands around his for a second, and then gently pull away so I can eat.

"What was that for?"

"For getting me."

"I think we get each other."

"I think you're right."

He grins, and his smile warms my bones. "After dinner, why don't we run out and grab a few movies to watch tonight."

"I was thinking the same thing," I say, digging into my salad.

Matt places his fork on the table and looks up at me. "The other day, I saw your journal on your bed. How's that going?"

"Faithfully done every night," I say, staring at him and waiting because I know there's something more to that question.

"Is there still a bunch of pages being filled up with Michael's name?"

"Michael who?"

He grins again. "I really hope that's the case."

I reach over and bring his hand to my lips, giving it a soft kiss. "It is. I promise you. The only name that has filled my journal for quite some time is yours. Well, Jack and Mary are in there, too, of course."

"Of course."

I want to tell him.

I want to tell him that the only space in my heart is occupied by him.

Chapter Fifty-eight

March 8, 1995

"I love the snow and I love the way it layers roofs in a white blanket of softness. In a couple of weeks, it will be gone and spring will come," I say as Matt and I stare out through his big bay windows with glasses of wine in our hands and full bellies.

"I can't believe that it's still snowing in March. But I love how you can see the smoke coming from the chimneys nearby. Tonight, even the stars seem as if they are shining brighter than I have ever seen them," Matt says as I rest my head on his shoulder.

"I think it's your turn to do the dishes," I say as I sit up to take a sip of my wine.

Matt looks back at the kitchen and sighs. "Isn't that what you said last Wednesday?"

"I was hoping you wouldn't remember. Okay, it's my turn," I say as I slowly stand up.

He touches my hand and I look down at him, seeing the love that he has for me reaching his eyes. "I'm not ready for you to leave me just yet. I think I need a taste of that wine that's on your lips."

"It that right?"

"It must certainly is," he says, gently pulling me back down to the sofa, and then moving his warm lips on mine. "Wine tastes so much better that way. I think I need more of it." His lips envelop mine as I slip my arms around him to bring us closer. "You know I love you," he adds, gracing my chin with the tips of his fingers and meeting my eyes in the soft moonlight.

"I didn't know you loved me."

"Yes, you did. But I'm not expecting you to say it back. I told you that we would take things slow, and I meant that, even if my heart doesn't want to."

I was afraid to ask him what his heart did want, afraid to admit how much my own heart aches for him. More than anything, I was frightened of what I saw ahead for us.

Marriage Lane.

I wasn't sure if I could take traveling down that road again without turning on Forever Boulevard. "Why do you love me?"

"For one thing, you're smart, courageous, and you don't let fear paralyze you. You don't give in to it. I love how modest you are. You understand that you have limitations, like when you took the car that Jack and Mary gave you."

"I love that car. I will probably drive it until it falls apart on me," I say with a fond smile.

"See, that's what I'm talking about. You get how to have much and how to have little, and you know how to enjoy both. I like how down-to-earth you are. It's refreshing. When I was in New York, I always felt like the people around me put on airs. It was hard to see who they really were. Laura was like that sometimes, but I didn't realize it until after we broke up. When she and I went out, we always did what she wanted to do. I'm glad that you and I haven't been like that. It's been the right blend of your likes and mine."

"So, you really like all those sci-fi movies I make you rent on Wednesdays?" I jokingly ask.

"I think we've learned how to create win-win situations."

"I wasn't always that way," I say. "I used to doubt myself and for a long time, I hated my skin. I called my hair nappy and was afraid to go after the things that I wanted. I have Jack to thank for who I am today. He pushed me to leave my comfort zone, to see my inner beauty, to feel my strength, to sing, and to remain humble and thankful for all of it."

He runs his hand through his hair and then says to me, "Jack has a brain tumor."

His words seem explode in the air between us as I slide to the other side of the sofa and stare of him. I place my hand on my heart and feel it beating rapidly as my mind struggles to comprehend the words that my ears just heard.

Cancer?

"How long? How long has he known? How long have *you* known?" I ask, feeling tears slip down my cheeks. I don't bother wiping them away.

"Since about three months before I came back to Atlanta. Mary called me and asked me if I would consider taking over the restaurant when the time came."

Mary and Jack knew that long ago and didn't tell me? How could they do this to me? They said I'm their daughter.

"How bad is it?" Matt runs his hands through his hair, but doesn't immediately answer, so I press, "Tell me the truth, Matt."

"It's terminal, Mýa."

I stand up and gasp in disbelief. "Did the doctors say how long he has?"

Matt gets to his feet, too, and wraps his arms around me. He lets a few of his own tears fall before answering. "The doctors gave him three to six months, but Jack is determined to prove them wrong."

"Why didn't anyone tell me? Is it because I'm not really—"

He wipes my tears away. "You know that's not it."

"Then what? Why am I just finding out?"

"Jack made Mary and I promise not to. He didn't want you to give up on pursuing a singing career to stay and help out at the restaurant. He loves you so much."

"Why tell me now? What has changed?" I ask, terrified to hear the answer, but knowing that I won't be able to take another breath until I hear it.

"The tumor is progressing faster. At first, Jack was only coming in to work the two days that you would be there, but now, he doesn't come in at all. He struggles every Monday to pull himself out of bed for our family dinners, and he's still insisting that Mary and I not tell you what's going on with him. You can't tell him that you know; it would crush him."

"I feel like screaming," I say, feeling like the wind has been knocked out of me.

"Then go ahead," Matt says, pulling me into his arms. "My shoulders can take it."

I place my head on those shoulders and feel the strength of his arms enveloping me. "How am I supposed to act like I don't know?"

"It's going to be hard, but you have to do it for Jack."

"Poor Mary," I say, lifting my head to look up at his face. Part of me hopes that I'll find something to convince me that this has all been just some sort of bad dream, and that in a few minutes, we'll go back to watching the icicles form on the trees outside, or the smoke climb up to the sky from the chimneys around us.

But of course, that's not the case. Instead of doing any of that, I spend the rest of these evening crying on Matt's shoulder.

Chapter Fifty-nine

A s I slip around the back of Jazzmyne's place and make my way inside through the kitchen, I can't believe how packed it is on this cold Friday evening. I wave at the kitchen staff as I head toward my dressing room.

My dressing room—I wouldn't have it if Jack hadn't pushed me.

It's taken every ounce of self-control in my bones to keep me from calling Jack. Part of me is angry that he didn't tell me about the tumor. The other part of me loves him even more for it.

Jazzmyne knocks on my door as I pull a box of Kleenex out of the bottom drawer and begin trying to clean myself up.

"We missed you at four today," she says as she looks at my swollen eyes. "What's going on? Why the tears?"

I can barely keep my emotions in check as she leans against the wall and listens as I tell her about Jack.

"I am so sorry to hear that," she says. "I know how much Jack means to you. He and his wife come here faithfully every Sunday with your boyfriend. It's like they're part of the family here."

"They are the reason I'm even here—Jack in particular."

Jazzmyne takes a seat in a chair next to me. "You know, right after I lost my husband, I had to perform in front of thousands of people. It was back when the band and I toured in Europe for a while. To this day, I can't tell you how I mustered up the courage to do so. But I will tell you that I know I did it for him." She gives my hand a reassuring pat and then looks around my dressing room. "This place was his dream, but it became mine. It's funny how life does that—teaches us how to love so much that we love the dreams of others. We allow their dreams to melt into our hearts and make a home."

"That's true. I'm sorry for being late and not calling."

She gives me a sincere smile. "I'm just glad you showed up; you could have stayed at home. So thank you."

I put the box of Kleenex back in the drawer. "Jack would kill me if I didn't," I say through a weary smile.

She stands up. "Before I leave, I thought I should warn you; your old boyfriend is here. He asked if he could come back here and speak with you, but I told him that you weren't here yet. Just thought you should know so you aren't startled when you walk out on that stage and see him in the audience."

My hands shake as I grab a bottle of water.

Michael is here.

As soon as the show is over, I make my way back to my dressing room. I saw Michael sitting in the crowd, just as Jazzmyne said I would.

He looked as good as ever.

When I hear the knock on my dressing room door, I instantly begin to think about all the things I want to say to him. One being, "I hope you got the ring I mailed you." I count to three, tell my nerves to behave themselves, then finally say, "Come in."

"Hi, Mýa."

I turn around to find Matt standing there. The moment I see the tears in his eyes, I know.

What it feels like as my body slides out of my chair and my knees hit the concrete floor, I don't know. What I do know is that the darkness encroaching on my vision overwhelms me, blocks out everything else. The agony that blazes within me won't be comforted, not even by Matt's touch as he sinks to the floor beside me and draws my shaking body into his arms.

The hurt in my kidneys is familiar. It was there before, back when Mama died. As tears stream down my face, I long for one thing.

Mama's Vaseline to heal the pain.

Chapter Sixty

—✦✦✦✦✦—

Matt and I sit outside Jack and Mary's house for what feels like hours. Every time I look at their front door, the tears come back and I remember that Jack will never come out from behind that black painted door again.

"We need to go in," Matt finally says.

"I know," I say, unbuckling my seat beat. "Let's go."

I find Mary sitting on the sofa staring at Jack's chair, and I have to force myself to choke down my tears and be strong for her.

"I'll go to the kitchen so you two can talk," Matt says as I join Mary on the sofa and take her hand in mine.

"I can't believe he's gone," she says.

"Neither can I."

I want to tell her how upset I am that no one told me about Jack's condition, but I know that now is not the time. Mary needs my comfort, not my reproach.

"I keep staring at that chair. Did you know that I hated that chair?" she asks.

My smile is faint, but my love for her, for Jack, never could be. "I didn't know that," I say.

"I remember when Jack brought it home. I thought it was the ugliest chair I had ever seen, but after I sat down in it one day, I could see why he had purchased it. It has great back support. I commented on that so much that he went out and bought me one a few weeks later. Whatever I wanted, my Jack gave me," Mary says, placing her hand on her heart. "He brought me so much happiness. He gave me so much love—over forty years' worth—and yet, as I sit here without him, that doesn't seem like enough."

I can't find the words to comfort her, so I sit and hold her hand. Finally, I ask, "How did it happen?"

"Jack had been sleeping all day. I assumed it was from the new pills they gave him, but when I went into our bedroom to wake him up so he could get ready for dinner, he didn't respond. I checked his pulse, but there was none, so I called 911. When the ambulance got here, they said Jack had died in his sleep." I watch as she struggles to hold back the tears. "I can't believe he's gone, Mýa. I keep going into our bedroom, staring at his side of the bed. Touching his pillow."

We both start to cry.

"Why didn't someone come and get me sooner?" I eventually ask.

"It's my fault. I needed time. I didn't call Matt until around ten. I'm sorry."

"It's okay. I understand."

Matt comes back into the front room carrying a tray with a couple of cups of tea on it. "I thought you two could use this."

"Thank you," I say as he places the tray on the coffee table and takes a seat in Mary's chair. "I'll stay here tonight."

"No," she says firmly. "You have a show to do tomorrow and another on Sunday. I'm coming on Sunday, like usual. Jack wouldn't have wanted me to miss it. He never missed your shows. Remember that. Even when he could barely move, barely talk, barely breathe, he was there."

"I don't think I can—"

"Yes, you can. You know how much your singing meant to Jack. This is what he would have wanted, and I won't have it any other way. Promise me that you will perform this weekend."

I slowly nod, but inside, I can't imagine going through with it.

We all sit in silence for a few minutes, staring at the walls. Staring at Jack's chair. Looking at all the things he once touched in this room. Things like the portrait that hangs on the wall, just to the left of the television. In it, Jack is wearing a black suit with a sky-blue tie, and Mary has on a white lace wedding gown that seems to flow down and behind her to the white and blue flowered aisle of the wedding chapel they were married in.

Jack not only touched that picture often, he loved it and everything that it represented.

"Jack didn't want anything big," Mary says as she, too, stares at the portrait for a moment. "So I'm just going to have the burial and then invite the family back here. He and I had already talked about it. I'll call and make the arrangements tomorrow; they should be open on a Saturday. I would like to have the burial by Tuesday. No sense in—"

Mary's tears cut her off, and as I watch each one of them fall, all I can do is cry with her.

Chapter Sixty-one

Margaret knocks on my dressing room door and then sticks her head inside. "Hey, great show tonight. I'm not sure how you pulled that off, considering everything that you're going through."

"It wasn't easy," I say.

"I'm sure. There's someone here that wants to speak with you. I didn't know how you would feel about it, so I thought I'd better check with you first."

I take a deep breath. "It's my ex, isn't it? Michael?"

"I think so."

"I saw him in the audience tonight and I'm pretty sure I saw him out there yesterday."

"What do you want me to tell him?"

I dab the corners of my eyes, wiping away the tears that had fallen just after I wrapped up the show. "It's okay, you can let him in. Just give me a few minutes."

"No problem. I'll tell him to wait five minutes before coming back."

I study myself in the mirror. *Am I ready for this?*

"Mýa."

I take a deep breath and then turn around. "Hi, Michael."

He looks...like before. Handsome. Time isn't going to change that.

"I'm so sorry. I heard about Jack," he says as he stands in the doorway wearing a pair of black dress pants and a white collared shirt.

"How?"

"Jazzmyne told me when I asked if I could try coming back here tonight. I was here yesterday, but I think you already knew that," he says, stepping into my dressing room slowly.

"I did. What do you want, Michael?"

"You. Us. All of what we had. I want it all back, Mýa. I know I don't deserve it. I know I don't deserve *you*, and I know my timing is horrible, but I had to come and tell you how I felt before I lost the courage to do so."

He moves further inside my dressing room and I feel as if all of the air has been sucked out of the space between us, until all that's left are memories of the past.

"I waited for you, Michael. I waited for you for months."

He closes the door and leans up against the wall next to it. "I know you did."

"Did you get my letter?"

"I did, and the ring."

I can see sadness in his eyes, so I have to ask, "Did you open the letter?"

He nods.

"When did you open it?"

He rubs his head and sheepishly looks down at the floor. "I read it the day I got it."

Anger rises up from my toes as I turn back around and stare at him through the mirror. "What did you do with it?" I ask before turning around again.

"I threw it in the trash."

My hand slams down on my table, making it shake. "Get out!" I say as the rage in my bones flares up inside me.

He doesn't move. "Look, you have to understand where I was coming from and where I had been. Things went pretty dark after that night. I—"

"You hated me?" I search his face for confirmation, but I already know the answer. "And now you, what? Love me again? Is this how this goes?"

"I didn't stop loving you, Mýa. I just needed time to allow the love I felt for you to help me push past the—"

"Hate?"

He pushes off of the wall and stands in front of me. We stare at each other in silence until he reaches out and tries to take my hand. I pull away and he heaves a disappointed sigh.

"I was hurting, but I didn't hate you."

"I can't do this with you, Michael," I say, looking anywhere but at him.

"Mýa, please," he says as he kneels down in front of me.

"I'm with someone else."

He drops his head for a second and takes a deep breath. "I know. I saw the white dude," he says as he looks back up at me.

"The *white dude*? What's that supposed to mean?" I ask as my body tenses up and I automatically get upset by his reference to Matt's skin color.

He shrugs his shoulders. "Nothing. Forget I said that. It's just the jealousy in me talking. It meant nothing, really. I'm sorry. I came to Jazzmyne's a couple of Sundays ago and saw him sitting with Jack and Mary, so I didn't stay." I feel my body relax some until he adds, "Do you love him?"

"I do."

"As much as you loved me?"

I take a deep breath. "This is not a competition, Michael."

"How can you say it's not?" he asks as he stands back up.

I stand, too. "Michael, you're too late."

"Prove it." He pulls me to him and presses his lips against mine. At first I don't respond, but when I feel his hands on the small of my back, all of the memories of us when we were together come rushing back to me, and my lips move with his. He pulls back just far enough to look into my eyes. "Tell me you don't still love me?"

"It's not that simple," I say, disentangling myself from him and already regretting that I even allowed that kiss to happen.

"You kissed me back, Mýa. I could feel the love you have for me inside you as I held you in my arms."

"I need you to leave, Michael, and I need you to do so now."

"I'm not giving up on us. I mean it. I was a fool to let you go." He reaches in his pocket and pulls the ring out. "This ring belongs on your hand and you belong to me." He places the ring on my table. "Love endures, remember? That's what you said in your letter."

Before I can protest, he kisses my cheek, then turns around and leaves.

How am I going to explain this to Matt?

I pick the ring up and put it in my purse.

Chapter Sixty-two

M ary and I sit on the sofa as Matt prepares dinner in the kitchen. "Did I see Michael at your show last night?" Mary whispers. I nod. "Why was he there?"

I look at her with tears in my eyes, and I can tell that she immediately understands without my having to say a word.

"I see," she says as she takes my hand into her own.

"We kissed," I say hesitantly.

Her eyebrow arches. "Oh."

"It was…a mistake. It was all a mistake," I say.

"So what are you going to do? I assume he wants you back."

"He does. Do you think Matt saw him?"

"He doesn't know what Michael looks like."

"True." I lean my head back against the sofa and let out a deep sigh. "I don't know how I'm going to handle this," I say, wiping the tears away.

"What do you mean? It comes down to which one you truly love."

"That's just it. I don't know. Michael had asked me to marry him, and I said yes because I loved him with all my heart and wanted to spend my life with him."

"And how do you feel about Matt?"

"You know how you have that perfect pair of jeans?" I ask, sitting up again.

"I think I know where you're going with this, but yes."

"You just love them because they fit you like no other pair of jeans can. It's like they were made just for you. That's how I feel about Matt. He's like my favorite pair of jeans." I sigh again. "This is so complicated."

"It's not complicated, Mýa."

"Okay, so tell me how to uncomplicate it," I ask, eager for her to just tell me how to fix everything and get back to normal.

"You be honest with yourself. Twenty years from now, when you're sitting at the dining room table of your home, which one will still be able to make you laugh? Which one will still make you feel like a giggling little girl? That's the one you give your heart to, and you do so because you know they will never give it back or do it any harm."

"When you look at it like that, it does uncomplicate the situation. Thank you, Mary."

"You're welcome. Now, as Jack would have said, let's go eat. We've got a long day ahead of us tomorrow."

Chapter Sixty-three

M ary and I stand in front of the burial site, and I take a moment to look around at everyone who loved Jack before we watch them lower his coffin into the ground. Michael and David are standing in the back of the crowd, but I can still see both of them. Searching all the other faces that stand before me, my eyes fill with even more tears. I smile when I catch sight of Jazzmyne, Margaret, and the entire band from work.

Mary doesn't seem to see anything else as she stares at Jack's coffin, and I see the fingers of her right hand resting protectively on top of her wedding ring.

She was right. Over forty years is not enough.

The wind blows softly as each family member says a few words, including Matt. When he speaks about how important it is to forgive, how vital it is to not let time and hurt keep you from the ones you love—from family—I can't help but cry some more. My heart reaches out to him as he speaks about how he wishes he had come home sooner, rather than waiting for trying circumstances to give him a nudge in the right direction. I want to hug him as he ends his speech by saying how happy he is that he and Jack forgave each other, and how he will never forget the things that Jack taught him growing up.

"Jack was not just my uncle. He was the greatest chef I ever knew because, like everything else Jack did, he cooked from the heart," he concludes, then walks over to Mary and hugs her.

It's my turn and I can barely do what Mary wants me to—sing. I feel tears raging down my face the moment I open my mouth.

Matt walks over and whispers in my ear, "I'm right here."

I inhale and draw strength from the fact that he's there, standing beside me.

"This is so hard for me," I finally say, exhaling as I look down into Jack's grave. "As many of you know, Jack was more than my friend. He was the father that I never had. We fought because he would never allow me to forget that I had something to offer the world. Jack pushed me to do things I never thought I could. He wanted me to become the person he saw inside me. Jack believed in me, even when I didn't believe in myself. He used to tell me all the time that I can't believe in love until I believe in myself. And he was right. Jack was always right. Sorry, Mary." I look over and see her nod with a small smile. "Jack loved to hear me sing. One of the songs that I would sing at our Sunday night dinners was 'Feeling Good' by Nina Simone. It was his favorite. Today, I sing it for him because that's how much I love him. I will do anything—*anything*—for Jack."

※

Food is everywhere, and people who didn't come to the burial stop by to pay their respects. Even Caroline Thomas—Jack's first love—stands in a corner with her black husband at her side. As I study her from the sofa, I can't help but think about how Mary is so much more of a real woman than she could ever be. It comforts my aching heart to know that Jack married his true love.

Matt walks over and sits beside me as I watch Mary smile through tears. "How are you doing?" he asks.

"Better than I thought I would. I think seeing so many people here that knew Jack is helping. It's like getting a chance to share their memories of him. Does that make sense?"

"It does." He places a light kiss on my cheek. "I love you, Mýa."

"I love you, too, Matt."

"Really?"

"Really," I say.

He smiles and then runs his hand through his hair.

"What's wrong?" I ask.

"Why do you think something is wrong?"

I reach out and weave my fingers into his. "Because you always run your hands through your hair when you're nervous or anxious about something."

"No I don't." I give him the side-eye until he deflates a little. "Okay, maybe I do."

"So tell me what it is," I say.

"I saw Michael at the burial. Mary introduced us while you were talking with his friend." He pauses for a second before looking me in the eyes. "He wants you back, doesn't he?"

"Matt," I say, looking around to see if anyone is listening to us.

He reaches up to run his hand through his hair again, but then stops and places it in his lap instead. "I know this is not the time or the place to talk about it, but I would like for us to do so sooner rather than later. Can you come to my place tomorrow?"

I agree, and he squeezes my hand before he goes off to find Mary.

Chapter Sixty-four

—⚡⚡⚡⚡—

Matt is sitting in front of the window as I walk into the main room of his place. My heart begins to pound as I put my coat on the hook and move to the sofa, taking a seat beside him.

"Hi," I say.

The love he has for me is easy to find in his eyes as he turns his gaze toward me.

"Hi," he says. "You want a glass of wine?"

"No, thanks."

The crackle of the fire that he has going is the only sound to penetrate our silence. Each of us seems to be trying to find the right words to start the conversation that looms over us.

"I don't want to lose you, Mýa." He reaches for my hand, but I can't give it to him. Not yet, anyway.

"Michael and I kissed," I admit.

He stands up and runs his hands through his hair, but doesn't say anything. I search his face, looking for anything that tells me that I haven't lost him.

"I didn't want to hide it from you," I say when the silence becomes too much for me to bear any longer.

"When?" he finally asks.

"He came into my dressing room on Sunday after the show." I stand up and go to him, hoping he'll hear me out. "I didn't want it to happen, and I hate that I allowed it. I'm really sorry, Matt."

"Are you still in love with him?"

I move so I can stand in front of him, rise up on my toes, and gently pull him closer until his lips almost meet mine.

"I don't want to kiss you until I know the answer to my question, Mýa. I need to hear it, regardless of what it is. My heart deserves it," he whispers.

"You're right. It does," I say, pulling back. I grab his hand and lead him back to the sofa.

"I told Mary that Michael and I kissed." I see the pain behind his eyes, but I know that I have to keep going. He needs to hear everything. "Mary didn't scold me. Instead, she offered me some advice, the kind of advice that Jack would have given me, too."

"What advice was that?" he asks.

"She told me to be honest with myself, and encouraged me to look twenty years from now, when I'm sitting at my own dining room table. She told me to ask myself who will be sitting there with me. Who will be the person that still makes me feel like a giggling little girl? That's the one she said that I should give my heart to because that's the one that will never give it back or do it any harm." I reach over and touch his hair. "I saw you, Matt. I'm in love with you, not Michael."

"Then marry me," he says.

We move closer, until space no longer exists between us. He meets my lips halfway, and when his touch mine, my heart says yes.

Still, I know he wants to hear the words fall off the tip of my tongue, so I say, "Yes, Matt, I will marry you."

We lock our fingers together and allow the moonlight that enters through the big bay window to dance in our eyes.

Chapter Sixty-five

—⁂—

May 24, 1995

As I stand in front of the hair salon, I can't stop thinking about how it used to be Mr. Johnson's gas station. The fateful night that took place here hasn't left my memories, but I feel the forgiveness that I've given myself in my bones, and it makes me smile—something I have never felt I could do any other time I've found myself standing in this spot.

I feel someone tap me on the shoulder, and I turn around to find Michael and Jenna staring back at me. I can't help but notice that they are holding hands.

"Hi," Michael says.

"I'll go wait in the car," Jenna says to him.

We watch her make her way down the sidewalk, then I turn to Michael and say, "I didn't expect you to be here."

"Me either, but Jenna thought it would be good for me." He looks back to see if she's in the car yet.

"She's right," I say. "You two look happy together."

"We just started dating," he says, allowing his gaze to drift to me again.

"Good. I'm happy for you. I really am."

"You look beautiful, Mýa. But then again, you always did." When his eyes begin to travel up my body, I place my left hand on my purse and put my ring on display. He notices and asks, "When is the wedding?"

"Next month," I say.

"It's a nice ring. Not bigger than the one I gave you, though."

It takes all of my self-control not to reach out and bring my hand across his face. Instead, I grit out, "This is the ring that Jack proposed to Mary with."

"I'm sorry. That was unkind of me to say."

I give him a feeble smile, but I know deep inside that he doesn't mean his apology at all. "Can't you just be happy for me?"

"I was happy when we were together. I still want that," he says, stepping closer to me.

"You are with Jenna, and I am marrying Matt," I say firmly.

"Does he know we kissed that night in your dressing room?"

"He knows. In fact, I told him, we worked it out, and then he proposed that same night," I say as I move back, putting space between us. I look over at Jenna and see the worried look on her face.

"So you're saying he's a better man than I am?" Michael asks, staring into my eyes like he's daring me to prove his suspicions right.

But I can only say what he should see—the truth.

"I'm saying he's the better man for me and the man that I'm going to marry. Let's not do this, Michael."

"Why not? I'm still in love with you."

"*I'm* not still in love with *you*, Michael. I'm in love with Matt, and I gave my heart to him. My whole heart."

Anger flickers in his eyes. "Why can't you give me another chance? I feel like I'm being punished for something that you did."

I shake my head. "There it is."

"What are you talking about?" Michael asks.

"You still haven't forgiven me."

"That's why you're marrying some other guy? Can't my being in love with you be enough for now? You wrote in your letter that it should be, remember?"

I inhale the warm spring air to give my insides time to calm down. "How is David?" I ask, hoping to move the conversation to something else, something neutral. But as his jaw tightens, I know that he's not going to let it go.

"I guess love doesn't endure, does it, Mýa? And now you're trying to end our conversation."

"I just think that it's better that we talk about something else."

He takes a deep breath. "Fine, if that's how you want it. David is good. He misses you."

"Michael, we're not going to continue this conversation like this."

He places his hands in his pockets and looks over at Jenna for a second. "Well, I better get going," he says before turning back to me. "By the way, Jenna told me that she read a press release about your record deal. Congratulations."

"Thank you, but the record deal wasn't just for me. My band was included as well."

"To think, the first time you walked into Jazzmyne's was with me."

"Bye, Michael. I can't handle this conversation anymore." I wave to Jenna and quickly walk away. As I get into my car, I look back at the gas station and realize that I can no longer come here. And for the first time, I feel like I no longer have to.

Chapter Sixty-six

—⟨⟨⟨⟨⟨•

June 17, 1995

Y ou started as an assignment for me, but became my way of
life—a daily task that wouldn't let me rest unless I'd shared my
innermost thoughts, be it at two in the morning or eight in the
evening. You have been my savior on dark and lonely nights.

You have been like a second mother, allowing me to tell you everything that happened during the long hours of the day, everything that
ripped my heart open with joy and laughter, or pain and tears.

No judgment you gave, only a listening ear to my scribbling. My wild
talk.

Frankly, I don't know if I would have survived this year without you.

I can't say that I love you; you are not a person, although I suppose
one can love a thing, too.

So I say to you, my dear journal, thank you.

You have been a good friend and my closet, as Jack once said.

Thank you for understanding. For understanding everything.

Even today, as I sit here with only minutes left to write in you, you
understand why I'm wearing this dream of white and lace, and why the
person I gave my heart to told me that he could love...*someone like me.*

Discussion Guide

1. Do you think Mýa could have done more to stop Zee? Or do you feel that Mýa's potential sense of loyalty to Zee held her back in some way?

2. If you were in Michael's shoes, would you have held Mýa responsible for what happened to his brother? Why or why not? Do you feel Michael should have forgiven Mýa?

3. Michael seems to believe in love at first sight. Do you? Why or why not?

4. Do you feel that Michael was supportive of Mýa, or too persistent in pushing her to sing? How so?

5. Mýa deals with self-esteem issues. Why do you think having healthy self-esteem is vital? What can cause women to have low self-esteem, and how can they rebuild it for themselves?

6. Seeking help from a professional counselor was suggested to both Mýa and Michael, yet both refused. Do you feel that talking to a professional counselor might have helped them or even saved their relationship? If so, how? What are some of the misconceptions people might have about getting help from a professional?

7. Keeping a journal was how Mary and Mýa shared their innermost thoughts and feelings. Do you feel that was fair to Jack or any of their other loved ones? Should they have shared their thoughts and feelings with anyone else, or were they entitled to their own private musings?

8. Mary and Jack often gave Mýa advice. Which piece of advice resonated with you, and why?

9. Do you keep a journal? If so, why? If not, is it something you might consider after reading this book?

10. Mýa fought throughout the book to forgive herself and find peace. Do you think she finally found both? How important is forgiveness versus peace of mind?

11. Which one did you feel was better for Mýa: Michael or Matt? Explain.

Acknowledgments

W riting a book was hard after two years of trying to get in the right headspace. It wasn't that my love of writing had waned, but the stories that used to crowd my thoughts at night as I slept felt as if they had made their home in the mind of someone else. While 2020 came with many ups and downs due to COVID-19, I will say that the "stay at home" time helped me to find those stories again.

I am eternally grateful for the love and support that my husband continues to spoil me with.

To my mother and my stepfather, both of whom never stopped believing in me: thank you.

To my mother-in-law, who gets more excited about me writing a new book than I do: thank you.

To my sister, who got upset when I told her that she would have to wait until this book was released to read it: thank you.

To all of my family, especially my Uncle Charles, who can't stop smiling as he tells everyone he knows that I'm an author: thank you.

To LeAnn Sellers: thank you for always having my back.

To my friends, who have been my teammates and cheerleaders: thank you.

To each of my coworkers, especially Yoshee Sodiq, Jerome, Daniel, and Jasen: thank you.

To my publisher and all those who assisted with bringing this book to life: thank you.

Finally, to all my readers: thank you.

About the Author

Born in Illinois, Marian L. Thomas wouldn't say that her first career choice was writing novels. She saw herself working as a journalist for a local newspaper. In college, she served as a sports editor for the student paper, and later as the news editor. But Marian's writing path took a detour when she drafted her first completed manuscript. Now, she can't imagine not crafting stories for women that bring characters to life—characters who face real obstacles, cross difficult barriers to find love, and discover all the wonderful possibilities that life can offer.

Marian has been featured on television stations such as Fox, NBC and CBS, and in many print and online publications including *USA Today*. She currently resides in Atlanta with her husband, enjoys a big bowl of popcorn every night, and believes that pasta should be a vegetable. Readers can stay connected to Marian through her website and active social media accounts, so stop by and say hello or join her mailing list for new release updates.

Website: www.marianlthomas.com
Twitter: @marianlthomas01
Instagram: marianlthomas09
Facebook: www.facebook.com/marianlthomasbooks

What does an author stand to gain by asking for reader feedback? A lot. In fact, what we can gain is so important in the publishing world, that they've coined a catchy name for it. It's called "social proof." And in this age of social media sharing, without social proof, an author may as well be invisible.

So if you've enjoyed *Someone Like Me*, please consider giving it some visibility by reviewing it on Amazon or Goodreads. A review doesn't have to be a long critical essay, just a few words expressing your thoughts, which could help potential readers decide whether they would enjoy it, too.

CPSIA information can be obtained
at www.ICGtesting.com
Printed in the USA
JSHW052230010621
15427JS00003B/193